Giddy-Up

Love Burns Series: Book Five

Isobel Reed

Giddy-Up
Love Burns Series: Book Five
Copyright © 2025 Isobel Reed
All rights reserved.

ISBN (ebook) 978-1-964636-44-3
(print) 978-1-964636-45-0

Inkspell Publishing
207 Moonglow Circle #101
Murrells Inlet, SC 29576

Edited By Toni Kelley
Cover art By Emily's World By Design

DEDICATION

For all the cowboy lovers out there.
If you're out searching for one of your own, just
remember: some will give you the ride of your life,
others might buck you off and try to trample your
internal organs. But the best ones? They'll stroke your
hair and tell you you're pretty.

ISOBEL REED

CHAPTER ONE

Riley actually gulped. What on earth was Wade Evans doing here? Outside her staff-issued trailer, flashing those goddamn dimples at her and turning her mind to mush.

Like it wasn't mush before he showed up.

Okay. Fine. So it was plenty mushy already. It had been ever since yesterday afternoon when she'd been strong-armed into attending Zach's wedding. Zach was the oldest of the four Evans brothers. But he didn't work on the ranch like the others. Wade did though. He also just so happened to be the second oldest brother and the man in charge around here. And Riley's brand spanking new boss.

Where the hell is Bella?

That was a good question. Bella was the woman Riley had met yesterday and was responsible for the forementioned strong-arming. Where was she? She hadn't signed up to be harassed by dimples.

"Did you hear me, darlin'?" Wade drawled, this time tipping up his cream Stetson with one finger. "Bella's running late, so you're gonna have to make do with me as your escort."

Oh, she'd heard him alright. Hence the near catastrophic throb in her ears. This was the problem with social anxiety, how was she supposed to tell people she had it if her mouth was too dry to make sounds? It also didn't help that Wade of all people stood there. Staring. It was difficult enough to talk to regular people, but put a six-foot two, hard-bodied, blue-eyed cowboy in front of her and there was a strong possibility she may never speak again.

"Riley?" he prompted.

Say something. Anything.

"B-But..."

For the love of God.

This didn't bode well for the rest of the day.

Her head shook and her eyes hit the ground. This was embarrassing. Stupidly, she'd thought she could do this. She'd even got dressed up. And swapped her glasses for contact lenses.

Idiot.

"Hey." Wade's hand shot out, and the next thing she knew, a cautious finger was under her chin lifting her gaze to his. "You okay?"

Nope. Absolutely not.

Another gulp. Her instincts were telling her to run and hide. She couldn't though. Not just because there was nowhere to run to. But because Wade was her boss. And she really needed this job. Which meant, she couldn't just shut the door, she'd have to use actual words to try and get out of this.

Frigging marvellous.

"I, uh, maybe –" *Come on.* She cleared her throat and tried again. "Maybe it's uh, maybe I-I should give it a miss."

There. Done. Now she could return to her book and pretend this whole day had never happened.

Just as she was about to take a step back, their gazes collided. And all of a sudden everything went quiet. Even her usual, slightly bitchy, inner commentary was silenced. Wade's head dipped and she watched in fascination as his gaze traveled down the length of her. When his eyes dragged back up, her belly clenched. But it didn't feel like her usual anxious stomach ache. No. This felt different. Warmer. No, not warm, hot. Really, really hot.

Something that she didn't recognize flashed in his eyes. "And waste this pretty little dress of yours? I don't think so, petal."

Petal?

His hand was out now, in front of her, palm facing up. It was as if he expected her to hold it.

Surely not? That would be madness.

"Come on, the best man can't be late."

He didn't wait for her to comply; he simply took her hand and ushered her away from the safety of her doorway. Her heart was beating so fast, she was worried for her rib cage. Maybe that was why she followed him. Her body took the lead while her brain was distracted by a possible medical emergency.

Just seconds later, they were walking hand in hand up the gravel path. The crunch of the dirt under her heels getting louder and louder the further they went. She couldn't think of a word to say. Which was normal. What wasn't normal though, was that *he* wasn't speaking. Not that she knew the small talk habits of Wade Evans, she didn't. But this wasn't how things normally went in social situations for her. She'd be quiet and awkward. And the nearest person in her vicinity would attempt a conversation, often by peppering her with questions, before eventually giving up. But Wade. Wade was giving her nothing. And by the looks of it, he was perfectly fine not talking.

This is weird.

It was. She couldn't decide if it was good weird or bad weird. On the one hand, not talking was her preference any day of the week. But on the other, a part of her might actually want to talk to Wade Evans. The beautiful, blond cowboy who she'd been actively avoiding this past week because he was just too beautiful.

Yeah. That makes sense. You've spent a week running and now you're ready to chit-chat?

Nothing was making sense today. Not the makeup she'd put on. Or the hour she'd spent curling her hair into big waves. Especially not the figure-hugging crimson dress she'd put on, that she went out and bought just this morning.

Who are you trying to impress?

She didn't want to answer that. Mostly because the answer was holding her hand and making her skin hot. And she really needed to focus on not freaking out.

Dream on. He's sooo out of your league.

As if on cue, a cold gust of wind smacked her in the face. The good old fall breeze reminding her that she should never be fooled by a bit of sun. Or in this case, chivalry. She needed to remember that. Remember who she was. Girls like her didn't get the guy. They certainly didn't get guys like Wade Evans.

As they approached the main house, which belonged to Wade's parent's, Riley had decided the silence was in fact, a good weird. It was exactly what she needed to try and compose herself.

"There you are," Matt hollered as he made his way out the front door and down the porch steps. "We've been looking all over for you. Oh." He stopped briefly in his tracks, confusion marring his tanned face before greeting her. "Hey, Riley."

Matt was another Evans brother, younger than Wade and Zach but not the youngest. Jonah had that title.

She realized then, as Matt's gaze drifted down, she was still holding Wade's hand. And the man wasn't letting go of her. Instead of dwelling on that, she pushed out a "hey" back. She liked Matt. He'd been the one to hire her as the ranch's new live-in maid, and for that, she was grateful. She also wasn't as nervous around him or Jonah, even though they'd all clearly inherited the devilishly handsome gene.

"Sorry," Wade replied, addressing his brother. "Had to go pick up Riley, where do you want us?"

Us?

Matt looked between the two of them. Clearly unsure about what was going on and what the hell Riley was doing there, holding his brother's hand.

You and me both, buddy.

"Right. Uh. Well, guests have started to arrive, so Zach wants us all up at the alter with him."

It was starting already? How long had they been walking? Granted the staff trailers were a good walk from the main house, but she wasn't that slow.

As if reading her mind, Wade was quick to question Matt. "Isn't it a bit early for all that?"

"The ceremony starts at two, man—that's in ten-minutes. Jesus. You really need to get a watch."

So did she evidently.

Riley switched off after that. She let the two brothers discuss logistics while her attention went back to her hand. The one Wade was still holding. She couldn't remember a time she'd held someone else's hand. Which was sad, because she kind of liked it. In a strange way, it made her feel safe. And she never felt safe. It was a very new feeling. A feeling she was only just starting to process as she was jolted back to reality. She was being ushered again. By that hand.

"Come on, petal, let's get this party started, huh?"

Why was he calling her petal? And what if she didn't want to get this party started? What if she wanted to run away to the nearest barn and hide under some hay?

The closer they got to the backyard, the more appealing that hay was becoming. There were already so many people there. Gathered in groups, hovering around rows of white chairs which had been decorated with pink ribbons.

Riley was led down the aisle next, across the white silk carpet placed on the grass. She was then led to a seat on the front row.

That's when the panic struck.

"You sit here, darlin', while I stand up front. I'll come get you when the ceremony ends. How does that sound?"

Terrible. Horrifying. My worst nightmare.

"I-I don't think I should be sitting here," she whispered,

surprising herself by only stuttering once.

"This is exactly where you should be sitting, petal. You're the best man's date, remember?"

Wait. What? Date?

After dropping that bombshell, she was treated to a quick kiss on the cheek before he was gone. Before she could argue. Before she could ask where else she could sit. Before she could say anything.

Like you'd be able to right now anyway.

That was true. He'd left her well and truly speechless. Again.

***

Bella found her during the reception. Riley had spotted her during the ceremony too. And she hadn't been late. Not really. Which made Riley suspicious. Either Bella wasn't all that interested in a new friendship, or she was being set up. With Wade of all people. Which didn't make any sense.

"So, where were you working before the ranch?" Bella asked before taking a sip of her champagne.

They were still in the Evans backyard, well, it was more like a field that happened to be located at the back of the main house. They were under the huge tent that had been erected yesterday for the rehearsal dinner, only today, it was lit up with rows and rows of string fairy lights and adorned with pink roses.

"Uh, motels. I used to clean motel rooms." Riley's grip on her orange juice glass tightened. It was easier to talk to Bella than Wade, but that didn't mean she still wasn't scoping out the nearest exit.

"Awesome. So, you've always been a domestic goddess, huh? Maybe you can give me a few pointers. Mr. OCD over there—" she nodded her head in the direction of her boyfriend, Luke, who was currently at the bar with Wade, fetching them drinks, "is a bit of a neat-freak. But ever since I've moved in, the house has gone from chic to *hurricane damaged hoarder home* real fast." Bella winked.

Why was this woman being so nice to her? Riley was giving her nothing. Not even coherent sentences. Yet, here she was, joking with her like they went way back.

"Uh, well, if you ever need a cleaner, I'm off on Mondays and Wednesdays."

Bella's cheerful smile disappeared in an instant, making Riley question herself.

Did I say something wrong?

This was why it was better that she didn't speak to people. She was always saying something wrong. Missing social cues. And was just really damn horrible at small talk, no matter how many books with embarrassing titles she read.

"You know I'm not trying to book your services, right?" Bella's serious silver eyes locked with hers. "Not that I don't think you're great at what you do, I'm sure you are, but I was sort of hoping we could be friends."

Friends. So she did want friendship. She started to panic again at the confirmation. Riley had never really had any friends. She'd tried a few times. But most people didn't have the patience to stick around for very long.

Riley gave the woman a small nod, trying her best not to look petrified as she answered. "Okay. Yes. I'd like that."

Back was that smile. Beaming and everything. "Cool. Me, too. So, Monday's and Wednesday's, huh? Let's do lunch on Monday, where's your phone?"

This time Riley didn't answer, instead, she pulled out her phone. And in no time at all Bella took it from her hands.

"I'm adding my number and saving yours. If I'm running late, I'll be able to call you and vice versa. How does one sound at Molly's diner?"

Riley had no idea who Molly was or where her diner was, but she nodded anyway.

Like Wade, Bella seemed perfectly comfortable with Riley's lack of actual words and continued to speak. "Amazing. I can't wait to introduce you to the other women, too. They're gonna love you."

Other women? What?

Before she had a chance to ask, Wade and Luke were back.

The men came bearing drinks. But Riley had no use for yet another orange juice. There was enough acid making its way up her throat as it was, it didn't need any more encouraging.

The drinks in Luke's hands went straight to the tall table they were all congregated around. He was far more interested in wrapping his arms around Bella and pulling her into him than his beverage. Riley watched on, transfixed, as he whispered sweet nothings in her ear. Causing Bella to giggle.

The couple's easy intimacy was leaving a mark. Making Riley feel some kind of way. It wasn't jealousy so much, well, at least she didn't think it was. No. It was something like longing. She wanted that. Wanted it so bad, but she knew deep down she'd never have it. And that sucked. Maybe she would take a swig of that orange juice after all.

Living life on the edge as always, Riley.

"We're going to go dance," Bella announced through more giggles before being dragged away by Luke.

Alone again, Riley twisted to face Wade. Her sort of date. He considered her for a moment and made a decision. Next thing she knew, he was placing their drinks on the table, including the almost empty glass he had to pluck from her clutches.

"Wanna dance?" Wade's hand was in front of her again, signalling a request for hers.

He wanted to dance…with her? Why?

"Don't worry, I'm not as bad as your face thinks I am."

Oh, shit.

Now it was her face saying the wrong thing.

Just dance with the man.

Maybe she should listen to her inner voice for once. If they were dancing, they weren't talking, not that she was killing it with her conversational skills or anything. But it would take a load off, wouldn't it?

Fuck it.

Her hand slowly outstretched. It was a measly attempt that meant it only made it a few inches from her side, but luckily, Wade took pity on her and met her halfway.

"Come on, petal." Her hand was now officially wrapped in his, and it was being tugged toward the dance floor. "It's time to sweep you off your feet. Or maybe...it's time to prove to you that I don't have two left feet." His head turned then, and she was graced with a dazzling smile. "I know—it's time to put our best foot forward."

What?

A small smile tilted her lips. He looked mighty pleased with himself as his head whipped back around and his attention went back to where he was leading them.

She had to admit, that despite feeling like she was on the verge of a panic attack for the past two hours, she was actually enjoying the hell out of herself. Wade was not what she was expecting. Nothing like it. She just assumed a cowboy so handsome, in charge of such a huge ranch, would be different. Standoffish maybe. A little cocky. She definitely didn't imagine he'd give someone like her the time of day. And she wasn't expecting someone so calm. Patient. Comfortable in his own skin. Someone who didn't need constant conversation— which was damn lucky. And someone, who when he did speak, managed to constantly surprise her. Because he was kind of an odd duck.

Like me.

Like her. But prettier.

As soon as they came to a standstill, Riley froze. The music was country. The two-stepping kind. Two steps that she definitely did not know.

Wade was way ahead of her though, pulling her into him and twisting until they were facing each other. Keeping hold of her hand, he lifted, until their arms were high and pointed toward the DJ booth. He then clasped her other hand and gently placed it on his shoulder. His very muscular shoulder.

Wow. Okay. That's super hard. Like, rock hard. That can't be normal. I bet he gets tension headaches.

Suddenly, they were moving, and her panic-filled eyes met his.

"It's okay, darlin'. I've got you." Wade dipped his head and nodded to their feet, forcing Riley to look down. "Step to the left, with just your left foot." She did as she was told. "Great, now, bring your right foot over next to it." Again, she followed orders and brought her feet together. "That's it. You're doing it. Now, just keep repeating that move."

Maybe two-stepping wasn't so hard after all.

Speaking of hard, being this close to Wade Evans in all his muscular glory, wasn't exactly helping her anxiety. Breathless terror was right around the corner.

Drama queen.

Yes. She was. And yet knowing, didn't help. Concentrating on her feet did though. So that's what she did. She avoided bright blue and focused her gaze downward.

It was working really well until a slow song came on and Wade stepped closer. Their joined hands dropping to the side.

"Wrap your hands around my neck, petal." His voice sounded deeper as piercing eyes held her in place.

She did as he said, immediately.

Should I be worried about how much I like being told what to do?

Oh, God. Maybe she had a kink. Was it possible to be a bit freaky in the bedroom when you hadn't actually been in a bedroom...with anyone?

Riley would have to ponder that question another time. Right now, her body was being pressed up against Wade's.

Dear Lord, is the man smuggling bricks in his shirt?

His stare still hadn't wavered, and despite the very real desire to look away, she had fallen under his spell. Strong hands that rested on her lower back pressed once more until she was plastered against him. Her head tilted back, while his chiselled chin dipped.

"What happened to your glasses?" he rumbled, taking her by surprise. Again.

"Oh, um, I-I thought that…" *What did I think?* "I-I, uh, I wanted to look nice."

It was the truth. She was trying. For him.

"Contacts and glasses don't dictate a woman's beauty."

"Oh," was all she said. Followed by more gulping. She was beginning to wish she wasn't so close. Or staring into his eyes. The pure intensity radiating off him was enough to make her shake.

"You, Riley," his voice deepened, "are a beautiful woman."

She tried to swallow again but it felt like there was something stuck in her throat. *Beautiful?* He thought she was beautiful. That couldn't be right. He's drunk. Yes. That must be it. The man had had too much whiskey.

"With glasses or without," he continued. "Although, I have to admit, I prefer you with the glasses on. They're sexy as hell." A crooked smile tipped his lips.

Beautiful? Sexy? Was she in some sort of alternate universe? Never once had Riley been called beautiful. Cute, once. By a relative. And sexy, well, that was almost laughable. There was nothing remotely sexy about her. She was the ultimate plain Jane.

Drunk, remember?

Right. Although, he didn't really look that drunk.

"Do you want me to get you some coffee?" she blurted, remembering that was how you sobered a drunk person up in movies.

"What?" Wade chuckled.

The man was laughing at her.

Wrong again, Riley. Idiot.

That was her cue to run. Her head dropped and she started to pull away. But he didn't let her get that far. His hand grasped hers before she could turn to leave.

"Hey," he tugged, "what just happened?"

Lie. Say anything. Just get out of there.

"I-I don't feel well, I want to go home."

"Okay, darlin'. I'll walk you." Concern began to crease his brow as guilt hit her full force in the stomach.

"No. I. No. I don't want that." Freeing her hand, she did the only thing she knew how to do. Guilt be damned. She ran.

CHAPTER TWO

I can't believe she fucking ran.

Granted, Wade didn't exactly have women banging down his door to date him, but Riley was the first woman to actually physically run from him. In heels as well. That signals commitment right there. She wanted to get away from him so badly that she was willing to risk breaking an ankle in order to do so.

Fan-freaking-tastic.

Almost a whole day had gone by since he was left stranded on the dance floor, yet Wade could still feel the sting in his chest. How could he have been so wrong? He had been so sure there had been something there. Something electric.

"Hey!" Matt bellowed before snapping his fingers in Wade's face. "Earth to fucking Romeo. Some of us are still on the damn clock."

They all were. They were completing final checks together today. It seemed like the sensible thing to do given the hangovers his little brothers started the day with. Three sets of eyes were better than one.

"Jesus Christ, man," Jonah chimed in. "What the hell is going on with you today?"

"He's lovesick," Matt answered for him. "He's hooking up with our new maid. Which reminds me, you think we need to get her to sign something to say she's not gonna sue us for sexual harassment?"

"Why would she do that?" Jonah chirped.

"I'm pretty sure *sex with the boss* is grounds to sue," Matt answered.

Oh, the joys of working with family. "I'm not having sex with Riley, you assholes." Wade shot them both the dirtiest look he could muster.

"No?" Matt leant back against the barn door, crossing his ankles as he eyed him. "Then how do you explain the handholding and the moony eyes? Oh, and the fact she was your date to your brother's wedding?"

"She was?" Jonah looked confused.

Wade sighed. "It's a long story, okay." A story he had no intention of sharing. "All you need to know is that we're not hooking up and she doesn't need to sign anything, so can we drop it?"

"You fucking like her!" Jonah laughed and pointed at Wade, before turning his attention back to Matt. "Think you're right, we're gonna need to get her to sign something. Casanova over here might as well have love hearts in his eyes."

He didn't have the energy for this. He wanted to go home and tend to his bruised ego in peace. Preferably with a cold beer and a good TV show.

But that wasn't happening either. Not yet. He had one more thing he had to do today. Something he'd spent the day dreading.

Just get it over with.

The sooner he did it, the sooner he could go home. So, with that in mind, he flipped off his brothers and turned to walk away. Ignoring the many, many slurs being hurled at him as he did.

Making his way over to the staff trailers, he may have walked a little slower than usual. He was in no rush to do what he had to do. Which consisted of two things. The first being to check in on Riley, in case she really was sick, though that was highly unlikely. And the second, well, the second thing was the one he was dreading. He had to apologise.

Stop whining and man up. You owe it to her.

His ego was going to take another beating, but that didn't matter because it was true, he did owe her an apology. For crossing the line. Sick or not, Riley clearly wasn't interested in him *like that*, so calling her beautiful and sexy, despite it being true, was a mistake. A big one. He was her boss. She was his employee. And although he hated to admit it, Matt was right, she could totally sue.

Sooner than he was ready, he found himself knocking on Riley's door and holding his breath. He waited. Then waited some more. He heard footsteps warily approach the door, but it remained closed. So he tried again.

"Riley?"

He knew she was there. But why wasn't she answering?

Jesus, what if she thinks I'm a fucking predator or something?

That thought made him sick enough to start talking, closed door be damned. "Riley? You okay? Just wanted to check on you, darlin', and say sorry about last night."

The door whipped open then, revealing a wide-eyed Riley. Like every other time he'd seen her over the past week, she managed to take his breath away. This time in sweatpants and an oversized shirt.

"Why are you sorry?" she asked.

Here we go.

He cleared his throat and blanked his expression. He needed to be serious. Professional. And put his tongue back in his head. "I'm sorry about the things I said last night, Riley. My intention wasn't to make you uncomfortable, which unfortunately, I think I did. For that, I apologise. It won't happen again."

"The things you said?" Her head tilted to the side, genuine confusion contorting her pretty face.

Was she really going to make him say it again? "Yes. The things I said. Commenting on your looks like I did. It was inappropriate."

"Oh." She went quiet for a moment. He could see the wheels turning. Finally, she asked, "W-what *was* your intention?"

"What?"

He watched curiously as her hand went to her wrist. Using her thumb, she began stroking her pulse point. It was an odd thing to do. But then, she was a bit odd. And he liked it.

When he met her dark eyes again, they were sparkling, a look of sheer determination boring into him.

"You said *my intention wasn't*, so um, what *was* your intention?"

He was slow to answer, unsure if this was a test. A test he was about to fail. Surely, she knew exactly what his intentions were. She was shy, sure. But she wasn't dumb.

"I think you *know* what my intentions were, darlin', but that—"

"I don't," she cut him off.

Seriously?

His face must have conveyed exactly what he was thinking because she went on, even though he could tell it was costing her.

"I'm not good at reading people," she rushed out. "I, uh, I'm not great in social situations."

She was still rubbing her wrist. Harder than Wade liked. She was nervous. Embarrassed. He realized then, that she really didn't know. Had no idea.

Fuck.

Fuck indeed. Where was that 'don't sue' contract when you needed it?

Hell with it.

He took a step toward her, his hand immediately going to her abused wrist. He replaced her thumb with his, gently brushing over her skin which just so happened to feel as silky as it looked.

"You honestly have no idea?" She shook her head in response, her red lips parting and her eyes growing rounder as he got closer. "You think I go 'round telling every woman I meet that they're beautiful and sexy?" She didn't need to answer, not when he got a good look at the innocence leaking out of her. "I don't, petal."

"S-so...why tell me?" Her voice was so quiet, he could only just make out the words.

"'Cause I couldn't bear the thought of you not knowing. That would be a goddamn shame, darlin'."

Riley drew in a shaky breath, but her gaze never left his. "So that was your intention—to make sure I knew?"

She really wasn't getting it.

So spell it out.

"No, sweetheart. My intention was to ask you out." He inched closer, forcing her neck to stretch back. "To take you to dinner." His head dropped as he allowed his breath to sink into her skin, his eyes not leaving hers as he said, "To convince you to kiss me." He ignored the spike in his heartrate and let his mouth go to her ear next, where he whispered, "To take you to bed."

He felt her quiver. A smug sense of satisfaction washed over him then. He hadn't been imagining it. He could hear the crackle in the air. Feel her pulse pound beneath his thumb. She wanted him just as much as he wanted her.

Thank fuck for that.

Drawing back slightly and seeing her flushed cheeks, reminded him to reign himself in. "Go to dinner with me, Riley."

It came out more of a demand than a question, but she nodded, nonetheless.

"You're off tomorrow, right?" He already knew the answer, tomorrow was a Monday, one of her days off.

She nodded again. This time, a strand of dark hair broke free from her bun and hung against her still very rosy cheek.

"Pick you up around seven?"

"Okay," she quickly agreed, looking like she'd surprised even herself.

Hell yeah. He'd bagged himself a date. With the woman

he'd not been able to stop thinking about since he'd laid eyes on her.

Who also looks like a deer caught in headlights right now.

Right. The taste of her citrus scent on his tongue should have been an indication that he was still standing too close. It was too tempting. And he needed to take it easy. And quit while he was ahead. Before she changed her mind. Or phoned a lawyer.

He let go of her wrist as he took a step back. But just as he was about to turn, he remembered something. "Are you feeling better today? You said you weren't feeling well last night."

"I lied," she stated, causing him to smile. Goddamn he liked this girl.

Wade nodded, he wasn't going to ask why. He didn't need to. Instead, he tipped his Stetson. "Sweet dreams, petal."

He was graced with a small smile as he backed out of her doorway.

Bring on tomorrow night.

CHAPTER THREE

A date. She was going on a date. Tonight. With the most beautiful man she'd ever seen. Who thought she was beautiful. And sexy. And wanted to kiss her and take her to bed.

Lord, have mercy.

She was in over her head. Way over it. For many reasons, but the biggest being that she'd never actually been on a date before. Ever. Then there was the whole stupid stomach ache thing she'd get whenever she was near Wade Evans.

And crippling anxiety.

Oh, yes. How could she forget? Dating required talking. Having actual conversations. Well, it was a good thing she had a few hours to practice. And she was going to practice on Bella, who she was currently waiting to arrive at Molly's diner.

Riley continued to fiddle with the straw in her soda. She'd arrived early, like always and chosen a booth in the very far corner of the room. She preferred having her back to a wall, she didn't know why, but she'd put all her money on it being another fun quirk of her anxious mind.

"Hey!" A holler from across the diner had Riley lifting her head. It was Bella, waving enthusiastically at her, totally oblivious to all the other diners staring.

I wish I was that confident.

Bella was stunning, so Riley wasn't surprised her looks

came complete with confidence. It was just hard not to be envious.

"I'm not late, am I?" Bella slid into the red leather booth opposite her.

"No. Um. I was early. I'm always early."

Riley was treated to an easy smile. "Good. Have you ordered yet?"

"Oh, uh. No, I-I was waiting for you."

As Bella began to ponder the menu out loud, Riley observed. Taking notes. Everything about the woman was so effortless. Her blonde hair cascading over her shoulders wasn't styled, nor was it messy. But it looked so good. Like she just woke up with hair like that. She didn't have much make up on either, just a touch of mascara and some pink gloss on her lips. Yet, she could still pass for model material. And don't get her started on Bella's clothes, how could jeans and a shirt look so damn fashionable? Life was so unfair. It took hours for Riley to just resemble a human.

Once they were done ordering, Riley decided there was no use dwelling on looks. There wasn't much she could do in a few hours anyway.

And he's already said that he thinks you're beautiful...and sexy.

She was still a little dubious about that. He could just be lying. To get her into bed. Men did that. A lot.

Like you care if he's lying?

Okay, so maybe she didn't care all that much. Not after the goosebumps he'd administered yesterday. She'd already decided she wanted him. Whether he was a liar or not. She was going to do something for herself for once. That was the point of coming to a new town in the first place. She was finally putting herself first. That meant going after what she wanted. And what she wanted was Wade Evans.

Maybe you should learn how to string a sentence together first— before you get ahead of yourself?

Yes. She should do that. It was time to practice the art of conversation.

As soon as the waitress was out of earshot, Riley

announced, "I-I have a date tonight. With Wade."

Bella's perfectly manicured eyebrows shot up. "Okay. Wow. Getting straight down to it then?"

What does that mean?

It didn't matter. What mattered was that she practiced. Possibly get some advice. Or at least some useful information she could use to help her.

"How many girlfriends has Wade Evans had?"

For the first time, Bella looked perplexed. "Oh. Well. I'm not entirely sure."

"Would you say it was a lot? More than five?"

Bella let out a short laugh. "Sorry honey, I've no idea. Maybe this is something you should be asking him? Also, really, does it matter? I mean, he's single now, right? Whoever he was with before, it didn't work out, so it shouldn't matter."

She was right. It shouldn't matter. But Riley's grand total of zero was mocking her. She felt like she needed to know what she was up against. Information was power.

"I've never had a boyfriend." Riley was getting good at this conversation stuff. She was sticking to the same subject. Sharing personal details. Having a back and forth. The authors of the books she'd read would be proud.

"Okay," Bella said slowly. "I take it that's why you want to know how many relationships Wade has been in?"

Riley nodded before taking a big sip of her soda.

"Right," Bella continued. "Well, y'know, *technically*, before I got with Luke, I'd never had a boyfriend either."

No. Fucking. Way.

"What?" There was no way in hell that Riley was hiding the shock on her face.

Another giggle escaped her shiny lips. "Yep. It's true. I'd dated, not much though, definitely less than five guys! But I'd never been anyone's girlfriend before…not until Luke."

Oh. Riley slumped back into her squeaky seat. It wasn't the same. She'd dated. Of course she'd dated before. What kind of freak hasn't dated anyone by the time they reached thirty years old.

You.

Obviously, apart from her.

Clearly sensing her disappointment, Bella went on to ask what was wrong. Something Riley didn't want to answer, but she had no choice. She was well aware that conversations didn't just end abruptly, they had to naturally segue to a new topic. And this wasn't exactly segue material.

"I've not dated either," she replied.

Bella also wasn't good at hiding her shock. So at least they had that in common.

"No one? Ever?"

"No."

"Does that mean…that you've never, uh, you've never—"

Riley took pity on her and shook her head in reply. Leading to more creases on Bella's brow.

"What about kissing, you must have kissed someone before?"

She could feel heat rising up her neck. The gravity of what she'd just shared was starting to kick in.

Oh, no. What if she tells Wade?

"Please don't tell Wade," she blurted.

To her relief, Bella began shaking her head. "Of course I won't. That's not my story to share." *Thank God.* "But, y'know, if you guys do get *intimate*, then it's probably better to tell him beforehand."

The idea of getting intimate with Wade really wasn't helping her flush that had now spread to her cheeks. It made her think back to yesterday, and the words he'd whispered into her ear. *Take you to bed.* She could still feel his warm breath and recall the shiver that went all the way down to her toes. She'd decided right then and there that was exactly what she wanted too. For Wade Evans to take her to bed. All she had to do was not fuck up tonight's date and any others that came after.

Yeah. You need help. Like, you really need help.

"Uh, Bella?"

"Yes, honey?"

"Do you think you could help me, and like, teach me?"

"Teach you what?"

"How to date. What to wear, what to say. Sex. Everything."

Bella looked like she was about to hurl, which was unfortunate because their food had just arrived and was being placed in front of them. It was only after the waitress left that her new friend spoke again.

"*Everything?*" Bella asked, to which Riley nodded. "Fuck it." She threw her hands up. "I can try, honey."

Riley would take it. She'd take all the help she could get.

***

To say the date hadn't got off to a great start was an understatement. They hadn't even got in the car yet.

"I'm so sorry!" Riley repeated. "Are you okay?"

Wade was not okay. He was clutching his crotch and he'd gone a shade of red that Riley hadn't seen on a human before.

"Yeah," Wade wheezed. "I'm okay."

This is why women shouldn't wear heels. They're dangerous. You can trip on gravel at any second and accidently injure your date.

"My hands…I thought I was going to…" *Facepalm the floor?* "Uh, fall and they just, they just…" *Smacked you really fucking hard in the balls.* "Shot out."

"It's okay." His voice still sounded awfully high. "It's fine."

His limp over to the truck told her otherwise. And the facial expressions he made as he gestured her inside didn't do much to convince her either.

"I'm sorry," Riley said again as she climbed into the seat.

After a nod and more assurance that he was "fine", Wade circled the vehicle and joined her inside. Other than apologising for the millionth time, she couldn't think of a thing to say, so she stayed quiet. It seemed safer at this point.

As she stared out the window, she noticed a sign signalling they were heading toward Goldacre. That was the next town over from Woodvalley Pines, she'd heard great things about the place from Bella, so she was hoping Wade had picked somewhere nice for them to go. And quiet.

"So…" Wade cleared his throat, his voice back to its normal pitch. *Thank God.* "What made you want to come and work in Woodvalley?"

Riley wasn't any good at lying, but she really didn't want to tell Wade the truth. Especially on their first date. The man didn't need to hear about her childhood.

So, what do I say?

She pondered. Maybe a bit too long because before she knew it, Wade was calling out her name. Likely checking she was still conscious.

"Um. Well. I wanted…" *To get away? No. Think.* "I wanted a change." *Yes. Perfect.*

"I get that." He nodded as he glanced her way. "Change is good."

Your turn, ask him a question. One from your book.

Right. "What are your hobbies?" That was a classic.

Looking at Wade, expectantly, she noticed him eye her, an odd look on his face. She had no idea what that meant but it was gone quick as he answered her question.

"Hobbies, huh, well I guess I get to do most of the things I love at work. Like riding, fishing, hiking. So on my days off, I like to just stay in. Watch a movie, read a book, sit out by my firepit with a beer. That kinda thing. How about you?"

This was better. This was how a date was supposed to go. He asks a question, she asks a question, and then repeat. Conversation table tennis at its finest. She was so excited. She was actually doing it. Kicking small talk's ass.

Go on then, answer the man.

Yes. Right.

"I'm boring, too. I like staying in."

Wade let out a short, sharp laugh. "Boring? Wow. Okay." *Shit.* "I mean, I would've preferred maybe *'a man of simple taste'* but okay, *boring* it is."

Great. First, she'd assaulted him, and now she was insulting him.

Good job, Riley. Are you going to steal his wallet next?

She was starting to wonder whether this date could get any worse. Fifteen minutes later, she realized it could.

When they'd pulled up to the restaurant, Riley could see full tables through the floor to ceiling windows. But she got out of the car anyway. There was always a chance they'd be led to another room. Wasn't there?

Apparently not. The perky teenage waitress led them right to a table in the centre of the crowded room. She was in literal hell. The place was every anxious person's worst nightmare. And she was slap bang in the middle of all the chaos. So close to the table next to them that within five minutes of being seated, she already knew the name of the woman's cat, when her mother was visiting next and why her brother-in-law wanted to quit law school.

Riley's thumb was on her wrist, rubbing ferociously, but the calm she normally got wasn't coming.

"You okay?" Wade asked, his elbows hitting the table as he leaned forward.

Her head shook and her heart raced. She was fucking this up so badly. She could even see the disappointment on Wade's handsome face.

I need to get out of here.

If she stayed, things would just get worse.

"Can you take me home?" Riley's voice was shaking almost as much as her hands.

More disappointment staring back at her. She couldn't stand it.

"Can I ask why?"

She didn't want to lie again. She'd already run out on him once with a lame excuse. But she also couldn't have the honest conversation she needed to have while her ears were pounding, and she was close to throwing up her chips and dip.

"I-I don't feel comfortable." It was the truth. A short version of it. And all she could manage.

Luckily, Wade didn't ask for more, he simply nodded once before rising from his seat.

"I'll pay for the drinks, do you want to meet me out front?" There was a coldness to his words. If she wasn't already shivering, she was certain the side of chill she just got served would have hit harder.

Nevertheless, he'd given her an out. One she was taking. Her nod was maybe a bit too enthusiastic as she got up and got out.

The drive back was tense. Riley wanted to apologise, explain, beg for another chance, but the anxiety attack she'd been fending off had found her. So instead of talking, Riley spent the next twenty minutes in Wade's truck with her eyes closed. Battling for control.

When they finally arrived back at her trailer, her attack had subsided. Just in time for the mortification to set in. Talk about the worst date ever. She couldn't get out of the truck faster. As soon as the vehicle came to a stop, she was thanking him and saying goodnight before running to her door. Yes. Running.

How the hell she was going to face him tomorrow, she didn't know.

That's a problem for future Riley.

CHAPTER FOUR

Wade just couldn't catch a break. He really thought he'd found something good. Something real. But no. It was just another freaking dating disaster to add to his massive collection.

Ironically, he was the one, out of all his brothers, who had spent his life searching for someone to spend forever with. Ever since he could remember, he'd dreamed of being a husband, a father, and one day a grandfather. Yet, he was the brother who was eternally single. The brother whose dates apparently couldn't even stand him long enough to get through a meal.

I should just give up and get some cats.

"Matt said something about you dating the new maid. Is that the chick you brought to the wedding?"

So much for peaceful silence.

Snapped out of his self-pity stupor, Wade twisted his neck to face Zach.

Zach had only just joined him on their parents' porch. Matt and Jonah were late. He had no idea why they still met there, the business belonged to them now and not their father, but the main house was where they all still congregated.

"Matt needs to mind his own business."

"I take that as a yes, then." Zach chuckled.

"Remind me again why you're not on your honeymoon?" Wade's eyes narrowed on his brother.

"Oh, it's like that is it?" Zach pasted on an annoying smirk. "You must really like this one if you're already dodging questions."

That was enough to make him sigh. He did, no, *does* really like her. But there was no coming back from last night. And it wasn't just the godawful date that was the final nail in the coffin, no, it was the fact that she couldn't even look at him for the whole drive home. That shit stung.

"It's not like anything, because it isn't *anything*," Wade clarified. "I'm not dating the new maid. End of story."

"Don't tell me you've blown it already?" Matt's big hand came down and slapped him on the back. Great. Goddamn perfect. "That was quick. Even for you!"

"So there is a story!" Zach laughed. "I fucking knew it!"

"You're late." Wade was back to dodging. "Where's Jonah?"

"Last I saw him he was challenging Old Bessie to a staring contest over on the south pasture." Matt laughed as he dragged a chair over and slumped down into it. "Seriously though, your date didn't go well?"

His brothers really needed to learn to read the room. Nosy-ass bastards. Wade's signature cream Stetson came off and was placed on his mother's wicker table. He ran a hand through his hair in frustration.

"I don't think it went well, dude," Zach answered for him.

Very observant.

Wade could only sigh. "Are we having this meeting or not?"

"You're changing the subject," Matt surmised.

"He did that to me, too," Zach added.

"The date that bad, huh?" Matt asked again, ignoring Wade's very obvious *shut the fuck up* face.

"Whose date was bad?" Jonah bellowed as the porch door swung open. "Shit. The maid?"

"Told you we need that contract." Matt sniggered.

Wade's head shot back as he slumped in his seat. He let his brothers get it out of their system. Although there were a few head shakes as they unashamedly joked about the sorry state of his love life.

This is what hell feels like.

This was the problem with having three brothers. No fucking boundaries and endless goddamn ribbing.

Despite the many questions, he refrained from divulging details of his disastrous date. He didn't need to give his brothers any more ammunition to mock him with.

"If you assholes are done..." Wade eventually interrupted. "We have a meeting to get on with."

A few grumbles later and to his relief, it was finally back to business. Which was lucky as they had a lot to discuss.

Jonah went over the monthly figures while Matt updated them on plans to move the cattle over to the north pasture. It was then Zach's turn to kick off the long-term planning portion of the meeting.

"The reviews from the guests are generally good, but we're seeing the same feedback over and over again," Zach started. "Food. We need facilities on site. And not just for guests, Ma is getting on, she can't cook for the ranch hands forever."

"So, what are we talking about here, building some sort of restaurant? We can't afford that." Matt chimed in.

"I'm not suggesting we set up some gourmet fine fucking dining Matt, but we need something. Like a cafeteria where guests and staff can both sit down and eat."

"You run the numbers?" Wade asked. It wasn't just a building they needed to consider—it was staff and food costs too.

"I have." Zach nodded while stretching to pull a piece of paper from his jean pocket. "It's not cheap obviously. But I think we'll be able to make the money we put in back within two years."

Wade took the paper from his brother and gave the

numbers on it a once over.

"Two years is a long time," Jonah declared.

It was a long time. But Zach was right. It was something they needed. And something they would need to sort out eventually, so why not now. Besides, the numbers he was looking at didn't look so bad.

"Why is the building cost so low here?" Wade asked. "Building from scratch is gonna cost a whole hell of a lot more than that."

A small smile started to spread across Zach's face. "We don't need to build from scratch. The red barn is just collecting dust brother, why not use that?" Wade's face must have said it all as his brother was quick to continue. "Think about it. It's halfway between the staff trailers and the guest cabins, right? It's big, so there'd be space for enough seating for guests and staff. And it's already got electric and water."

His big brother made a good point. Using an existing structure would not only cut costs but mean they'd have the cafeteria up and running sooner. And the sooner it was open, the sooner they could start making their money back.

"I like it." Wade nodded. "What do you guys think?" he asked, turning to Matt and Jonah.

A few chin lifts later and it was agreed. Now all they needed to do was plan the next steps. It was going to be a long night.

***

It had been six whole days and Wade still hadn't faced Riley. He was a coward. And he didn't care. Over the past week, Matt had taken pity on him and looked after the guests so he wouldn't have to venture anywhere near the cabins. But now it was Monday. Back to reality. Luckily for him, it was Riley's day off, so he had one more day to sulk.

So far, the morning was going well. He was on his way back from a trail ride with Bill and Sue, an older couple currently staying at the Evans ranch. Guest activities like this were what Wade lived for. Sometimes he couldn't believe he was making money riding, fishing, and hiking all day, it was like he was the one on vacation. Especially after a lifetime of cattle ranching.

Wade drew in a deep breath, the crisp fall air filling his lungs as he let his eyes flutter closed. It was his favorite time of year. Not just because shades of red and orange adorned the trees, but because of what it signalled. Shorter days and longer nights. Cool breezes and visible breath. Damp soil and dew-kissed grass. Pumpkin patches and cozy nights in.

"What a perfect way to start the day," Sue chirped from behind. "I told you we need to get horses, can you imagine, we could do this every morning."

"And where are we going to keep these horses, dear?" Bill chuckled. "Or ride them. Heritage Park is nice and all, but I'm pretty sure we're not gonna want to take two horses down the freeway to get to it."

Wade held back a smile as Gypsy, his coffee-colored mare slowed to a trot.

"I hope you guys are hungry." Wade turned to the couple. "Ma's got a breakfast spread with your name on it up at the house."

God bless his mom.

After an excited "can't wait" and "yes please" from Bill and Sue, Wade turned back and continued to lead them up the hill toward the stables.

But as the old wooden structure came into sight, his stomach dropped.

Seriously?

Riley. There she stood. Long black hair blowing in the breeze. Looking like a sexy, nervous, delicate flower in figure hugging blue jeans and a fitted black sweatshirt. All the while switching between straightening her black rim glasses and rubbing her wrist ferociously.

So much for that one extra day. It was time to face the music.

CHAPTER FIVE

Are you freaking kidding me?

This was stupid. Riley already knew Wade was going to arrive by horse. I mean, she was standing outside the frigging stables for God's sake. But holy hell. He was really riding that horse. Like, really riding it.

This is why women fantasise about cowboys.

Now she was one of them. But who could blame her. What woman could resist thick, muscular thighs wrapped in denim. Stretched plaid trying it's hardest to contain the kind of muscles only manual labor could sculpt. And let's not forget those damn dimples that even Wade's tipped Stetson failed to cast a shadow over.

You can do this.

Couldn't she? As the three horses before her came to a stop, she was beginning to doubt herself again. She was very much aware that Wade had been avoiding her for a week. Matt never dealt with guests, then all of a sudden there he was, taking over duties only his older brother usually dealt with. It wasn't a coincidence.

Wade expertly jumped down. Even that was sexy.

Control yourself.

Thirty years with no sex, and *now* her libido decides to make an appearance. *Really?*

Bright blue eyes hit her like a bolt of electricity. "Riley," he greeted. "Give me a minute to put the horses away and I'll be right with you, darlin'."

She nodded. And tried her best to swallow down her fear.

Her nerves didn't ease as he directed Bill and Sue to the main house, or when he slowly led the horses one by one into the stables. When it was time to take Gypsy inside, Wade's horse, Riley decided to follow him into the wooden shack. Before she changed her mind.

Once the chocolate beast was safely tucked away, she jumped right into it. "Um, I know I'm probably the last person you want to talk to...but—" she started but was swiftly cut off.

"Why would you say that?" His whole body twisted until she had his full attention.

She managed to push out another "um". Damnit. She hadn't prepared for that question in advance.

"Why would you be the last person I want to talk to?" he asked again, this time taking a step closer. Close enough for her tongue to get its first taste of his musky leather scent.

"I know you've been avoiding me," she said meekly.

Wade considered her for a second, his hand slowly going to his hat. Carefully, he pulled it off, revealing ruffled blond strands as he placed the Stetson on the top of the feed bin. His gaze never left hers as silence descended. But the quiet didn't bring calm. The air was charged with an intensity she'd never experienced before.

Riley couldn't take it anymore. She needed to say something to break this spell. Or at least break the concentrated eye contact that was starting to make her palms sweat.

"I owe you an explanation," she announced. When Wade's stare didn't falter, she decided to continue. "So, I, uh, I wrote one down for you." Pulling her crumpled paper from her pocket, she didn't miss that her hands were shaking.

Wade's head tilted. "You wrote down an explanation?"

"Yeah. I-I uh, sometimes my words come out wrong or uh, jumbled and I...I don't want these words to come out wrong."

More silence. More staring.

Her eyes shot down to the piece of paper she'd managed to uncrumple. Right. *Here goes nothing.*

The only problem was, nothing came out. She suddenly felt overwhelmed. Did he think she was silly for writing her explanation down? Was this going to be the final nail in the coffin? Should she just not say anything?

Or maybe I should just quit.

"So, do I get to hear what you wrote?" Wade's question brought her gaze up again. Having his eyes on her was no less intense but his expression had grown softer. It was enough to make her talk. Or at least try.

She looked back at the paper and began to read. "Our date was bad. And I'm so sorry. I take full responsibility. I guess you've probably noticed already that I'm a bit awkward...and I say weird things."

"No," Wade declared. Shocking her enough that she tore her attention away from her notes.

"No?" she repeated. He lies.

"No, petal. You're perfect."

Huh?

"I'm not perfect." She vehemently shook her head.

Wade took a step closer; his forefinger going to her chin as he nudged her until their gazes were entwined. "Well, I think you are. Why do you think I asked you out?"

"I-I have social anxiety," she stuttered.

"And?"

"What do you mean *and?*" Did he hear her? "I had a panic attack on our date."

"Okay."

Okay? Riley needed her notes. This wasn't how this was supposed to go. He was supposed to listen to her read everything she'd written. Accept her apology. Ask her on a pity date, where she would throw herself at him, he'd feel sorry for her, she'd lose her virginity and then she'd avoid him. It was all planned. But he was distracting her.

"I take it that was why you went quiet on the drive home?" He was taking this so well.

I don't think he's blinked once.

Or looked at her like she was a freak.

Shitballs. That makes me like him even more.

"Yeah. Uh. The restaurant...there was just too many people there and, and, it was so loud and we were sat right in the middle of everything. It was...it was just..." she trailed off.

"Too much?" he finished for her, allowing her to nod her agreement. "I get it. Let me try again."

She was supposed to beg. This was not begging. Is *he* begging?

"You still want to?" *Just say yes, you idiot.*

It didn't escape her notice that he was still touching her. Or that he'd somehow managed to inch even closer. "I still want to." His fingers skimmed her jaw, making her shiver. "But what about you...is that what *you* want, Riley?"

There were so many things she wanted right now. And the way he was saying her name, all deep and rumbly, was making her want them all at once. Her body was definitely more than ready to take what it wanted too. That was the only explanation as to why she decided to close the very small distance between them, her head shifting back as his own head dipped. But as her nose lightly brushed his, even she was surprised by her own blatant want.

Hot breath skimmed her lips, making them tingle. "Tell me what you want, darlin'."

Everything.

It was starting to become hard to breathe. For a moment, she wondered if she was on the verge of another panic attack.

No. This wasn't panic. It was something else. She felt restless. Hungry. Her body not quite knowing what it is she wanted but she craved it anyway.

"I—" she whispered, before letting her lips brush over Wade's angular jaw, the sting of his sharp stubble making her mouth dry and her panties wet.

"Say it," he demanded, his voice deeper than she'd ever heard it before. "Say it, and I'll give it to you, Riley."

That sounded like something she should definitely do.

Don't fail me now trusted vocal cords.

Unfortunately, the universe had other ideas on how it wanted Riley to spend her day off. That was made loud and clear as Matt abruptly pushed through the stable doors. "There the fuck you are."

Riley and Wade both launched themselves backward quicker than lightening.

"Oh, shit. Sorry. I didn't mean to…um, interrupt." Matt failed to hide the humor in his voice.

Talk about awkward.

Time to leave.

Good thing that running away was her special skill. She tried for a smile as she squeezed past Matt on her way out, but she very much doubted it conveyed any sort of cheer.

As she stepped outside, it was hard to tell if she was shivering or cringing.

I'll worry about that later. Time to get the hell out of here.

But before she could speed walk to the staff trailers, Wade caught her hand, pulling her to a stop and spinning her around.

"Tonight," he stated. "Tonight, I want a redo." Her head was nodding before she'd even had time to process his words. "I'll pick you up at seven?"

She was still nodding. Seven it was. Now it was time to run. Which is exactly what she did next.

***

Wade really wasn't kidding when he told her they weren't going far. Driving her to his house though was a bit extra, they so could have walked.

As he led her into the backyard, her smile quickly went from a shaky, nervous wreck to a huge, pearly white grin.

"You like it?" he asked from beside her.

Hell yeah, she liked it. He'd set up a table for two on his patio, complete with candles, wine glasses and a bottle of orange juice on ice.

"I noticed at the wedding that you didn't drink...so I thought we could stick with juice tonight." Was that apprehension she heard in his voice?

She turned to him then, the elation she was feeling managing to settle down the butterflies in her stomach. "Thank you. No one's ever...thank you."

The dimples were back, making her knees weak and waking up those blasted butterflies again. "I'm glad you like it, petal. Here..." He pulled out a chair and ushered her to sit. "Take a seat and I'll start bringing the food out."

Good. A minute to herself. Maybe she could use it to get her shit together. *No chance.* Yeah. That's what she thought.

She'd been on edge all day and she was blaming Wade's jaw. The moment her mouth met stubble; she'd been feeling him on her lips ever since.

Reaching into her jean pocket, she carefully pulled out the paper from earlier and placed it on the table. Yes, she'd brought her notes. Just in case. She hadn't got to read out her whole speech earlier and if the subject came up again, she wanted to be prepared. Speaking of which, she had time for one last pep talk.

Okay, Riley. Remember to ask questions. Fill silences. Maintain eye contact. Oh, and try not to say anything weird.

She totally had this.

Wade didn't take long to return, and with him he brought two plates piled high with what looked like lasagna.

Amen.

"I figured you can't go wrong with pasta, right?" Riley's gaze was pasted to Wade's smile as he lowered her plate to the table.

He was right. You can't ever go wrong when there is

pasta involved.

"Did you make this?"

Look at you asking questions and shit.

She was killing it. Not a stutter in sight.

"Yeah," Wade said as he took his seat opposite her. "I actually really love to cook. I don't do it as often as I'd like...mainly because it's not as fun cooking for one."

"You can cook for me anytime," she declared as she took in the sight of cheesy delicious goodness and began filling her fork.

"Oh, yeah?" Her eyes shot up, just as she'd shoved a huge amount of pasta in her mouth. His voice had dropped an octave again. It was back to the scratchy sexy pitch from the stable. "Does that mean I've already earned a second date?"

"What?" she muffled as she tried her hardest to swallow quicker.

"You just invited me to cook for you *anytime*." He chuckled. "I take it that means the date is going well?"

Of course. Multi-layered meanings. She was bad at spotting sentences that could have multiple interpretations. You'd think someone so anxious would think before she spoke, over-analyse everything she said, but no. Riley did the opposite. Especially when she was trying her hardest to speak in full sentences. She usually went with the mantra all words are better than none.

This time she finished chewing before she spoke again. "I, um, I..." Damnit. It was going so well. Suddenly, she remembered the letter. Picking it up, she was about to start reciting it when Wade interrupted.

"You brought notes again?"

She nodded.

"Can I?" His hand stretched across the table as she hesitated. "Please?"

She gave in. Paper passed; she waited anxiously as he read every word. But she didn't need to worry. When his eyes met hers again, all his features had softened.

"Thank you for sharing this with me," he said, passing her back the paper. "I don't want to ever do or say anything that makes you feel uncomfortable, darlin', so promise me you'll tell me if you ever feel that way?"

"Sometimes it's hard to say it," she whispered, her gaze dropping to her plate.

"I get that. Maybe we should come up with a sign then, like, if you bite your lower lip then I know you need to get the fuck out of wherever we are."

That made her giggle. A full-blown girly giggle. Her eyes were back on him now and she was forgetting to be nervous. "Does that mean I get a second date?" she teased, throwing his earlier comment back at him.

Wade's throaty laugh was glorious. And she couldn't help but feel proud she'd caused him to convulse.

I'm a goddamn dating master.

By some miracle, Riley was actually starting to relax. Enough to dig back into her dinner and even instigate a new conversation.

"I actually love to cook, too," she said in between bites. "Yeah?"

"Yeah. My dad taught me. He'd take me fishing every Sunday, then we'd go home and cook what we caught. He made the best smoked trout." The thought of those Sunday's still brought a smile to her face.

"Well, I know what we're doing on our second date now."

"What?" Her head tilted with the question.

"I'm taking you fishing. Then, we're gonna come back here and make us some smoked trout."

"Really?" she squeaked, not at all hiding her excitement.

"Really." He was giving her that look again. The one from this morning. The one that made her heart jump. "You know, we're going to be building a restaurant on-site. It's going to be in the old red barn."

"You are? That's so awesome. Are you going to do farm to table?"

"Farm to what now?"

"Farm to table," she repeated. "It just means you use what you have here on the ranch, like meat from your cattle, fish from the river, freshly grown vegetables…that kind of thing. It's pretty trendy right now, and slightly hipsterish, but I think it's a cool concept and it can actually keep food costs down."

After that, conversation got so much easier. Mostly because for once, she had so much to say about food. They talked more about the benefits of setting up a farm to table restaurant and she told him all about the article she'd read about the sustainability aspect of it. She fully geeked out when they discussed the environmental impact and at one point she might have even offered to be the chef. She was only half-joking. But still, she mentally congratulated herself for making Wade laugh again. On purpose.

It was the perfect night. They talked about food. They ate food. And she had the best view in town. Wade's dimples.

The date was going so well, she forgot to try and pretend to be normal. Her freak flag was flying all over the place, but Wade either didn't seem to notice or didn't care. She was obviously hoping for the latter.

Before she knew it, the date was over. She'd done it. She'd made it through dinner and enough orange juice to inflict some serious heartburn on most people. And she was okay. More than okay. Nerves were still bubbling beneath the surface as they walked toward her trailer but there was something else simmering too. Anticipation. And it only got stronger as they came to a standstill under the dimly lit walkway.

Despite the chill in the air, she was burning up, and she had no doubt a crimson flush was creeping up her neck.

This is where you throw yourself at him.

That was her plan. Or at least that was what she'd told herself. But Riley was beginning to realize that it had one major flaw. She could barely move let alone fling her body anywhere.

Being glued to the gravel didn't seem to matter though. Not when Wade had no problem getting closer. So close she was worried he could hear how fast her heart was pounding.

"You're biting your lip, petal." His gaze darkened. "I'm trying to decide whether you want me to kiss you or get you the fuck out of here."

This was it. Time to be brave.

Her mouth opened and for a second nothing came out. When she did speak, her words were hurried. So fast out of fear she'd change her mind.

"I don't want you to get me the fuck out of here."

He got the message. Loud and clear. Because within mere seconds, Wade's head dipped, and his expert lips captured hers with ease.

This was nothing like when Tommy Anderson smacked her lips and ran away in fifth grade. Her one and only kiss. And it certainly wasn't like in all those rom coms she watched, when the couple exchange sweet smiles before tenderly embracing under the starlit sky.

This felt so much different. Dangerous. Overwhelming. Riley's neck stretched back as Wade pushed her mouth wider. As his tongue slid inside, a noise she didn't recognize vibrated down her throat. Was that her?

She didn't have time to care if it was as his hand went from cupping her cheek to fingering her hair. He was directing her, angling her, so he could get deeper. Every swipe of his tongue making her insides heat as more sounds filled the night. Charging the air and making her body shake.

Too soon, he pulled back. But he wasn't done with her. His teeth clasped her lower lip as choppy breaths warmed her skin.

"Fuck," he hissed.

Oh no. Was that a good fuck, or a bad fuck? Riley's lust drunk brain cells started to wake. As the haze cleared, she was left feeling self-conscious. She'd never done this before, what if she was bad at it?

"You taste so goddamn good." Wade tugged at her lip. Pulling her into him again. A moment later, his mouth was back to covering hers.

It was a good fuck!

There was no time to celebrate. Not while she was trying her best to keep her balance as Wade's big body was propelling her backward. It was only once she was up against the door that she started to relax. Her brain embracing the fog as a wall of hard muscles pressed into her.

One hand was still in her hair, moving her to his will, while the other was on her hip, holding her in place. She was surprised at how good it felt. To be at his mercy. To let him do what he wants. Take what he wants.

Imagine what he'd be like in bed.

It was hard not to imagine as their kiss turned more urgent. And everything began to pulse. It made her feel brave enough to touch him. Her hand went to his side, her fingers tentatively digging into the fabric of his shirt as she got her first feel of what was underneath it.

Lord almighty.

"Whoa!" a deep voice called out.

They both startled. Wade jumped back a full step before turning to see who was there.

"Uh," the voice coughed. "Uh, sorry boss, I didn't mean to—" Riley turned to see her trailer neighbour Lance. He was one of the many ranch hands that helped keep the place running.

Her gaze darted between the two men; by the looks of it, she wasn't the only one feeling ridiculously awkward.

"It's fine, Lance." Wade nodded before clearing his throat. "I was just dropping Riley home."

And kissing the hell out of me.

Lance nodded back. "Great."

Apparently, they were all pretending she hadn't been pinned up against her trailer door moaning into the boss's mouth. Well, that was just fine by her.

47

"Anyway," Wade went on, "it's getting late. I should get going. Early morning and all that." *Boo!* "Lance," Wade offered the man a chin lift before turning to her. "Riley." He smiled. "Y'all have a good night now."

She watched him quietly as he turned to leave and couldn't help but feel disappointed. It was her first ever kiss and instead of doing it again, she was left standing with Lance. The teenage ranch hand who was definitely gawking at her.

"Um. Night," she squawked before hurrying inside.

Riley didn't get far, immediately slumping back against the door. "What now?" she mumbled to herself.

She had no fucking idea.

CHAPTER SIX

Wade couldn't concentrate. Every thought he'd had all morning always led back to Riley. It was pathetic. They'd had one date. With one kiss. And there he was, pining. Like a lovesick puppy.

But what a date. And what a fucking kiss.

It was true. The date, the conversation, the way she was looking at him. It was all amazing. But that kiss…that kiss was unbelievable. It felt raw. Messy. And slightly feral. He couldn't even remember the last time he'd had a kiss that passionate. Which meant he probably never had.

"Word on the street is that you hooked up with Riley last night," Matt bellowed as he sauntered toward him.

Damnit, Lance.

Wade ignored his brother's approach and continued to put away the fishing equipment from this morning's trip.

"I take that as confirmation." Matt chuckled as he slid up next to him and began handing him fishing rods.

"Take it as whatever you want. What are you doing all the way out here anyway?"

They were down by the river in their brand-new storage cabin. They'd built it this summer, so they didn't have to keep lugging equipment down to the river every time guests wanted to fish. Complete with outdoor seating and insulated bins containing bottled water, it also doubled up as the perfect place for a pitstop for hiking guests.

"I was looking for you, Romeo."

Wade snorted as he locked up the cabinet. "So you can bust my balls in person?"

"Sure. That and I just spoke to Joey about the barn conversion. He reckons he can make a start now, before the weather turns. Get the exteriors sorted so we can focus on the interiors over winter."

That was good news.

"I take it he's charging a premium for the rush job?" Wade turned to Matt and gestured him outside. His brother followed him out and onto one of the wooden benches.

"All taken care of. He's cutting us a deal and I got Jonah to sign off the figures."

He was impressed. His little brothers had come a long way since they all took over the ranch two years ago. They'd only been open to guests six months but thanks to the hard work they were putting in, they'd already made most of the money back they'd put down.

"Good work." Wade nodded. "So I don't need to do anything?"

"Not right now, no. But at one point you'll need to work out the layout for the kitchen, y'know, pick out appliances and shit."

That made him laugh. "Pick out appliances and *shit?*"

His brother threw a punch to his arm. "You know what I mean. You and Zach are better at all that stuff, so it's all yours."

That was fine by him.

Maybe I could take Riley along to help? She did mention she loved to cook.

He was doing it again. He hadn't even lasted a minute without thinking about her. Matt clearly spotted weakness, too. He had a giant smirk pasted on his face.

"So, I take it the maid gave you a second chance?"

It was rare that Wade ever wanted to talk to his brothers about his love life. But last night he felt something he'd not felt before. He was excited and he wanted to talk about it. And the sad truth was that he didn't have anyone else to talk to. Working seven days a week his whole adult life didn't leave much time for friendships.

"Between us?" Wade asked and waited for Matt to nod. "I really like her."

His brothers smirk softened. "Happy for you, man." Matt paused for a moment. "She's sweet and everything. But, y'know, she's a little…"

"Different?"

"Yeah. She's a little *different*. You gonna be okay with that?"

Wade understood what Matt was trying to say, not so eloquently. Riley didn't just come across shy, she was skittish too. Maybe even a little fragile. And definitely unlike any of the women he'd previously dated. But that was part of what he liked.

"Oh, I'm more than okay with that, the real question is…is she?" The million-dollar question.

"What do you mean?"

"I mean…she's ran out on me twice now, in the space of a week. How long is it gonna be before she runs again?" *And next time it's going to hurt even more.*

There was no doubt in Wade's mind that it was going to happen again. Not after reading her note. Just like her, anxiety in any form was unpredictable. And that lack of control was going to be an issue. Especially for him. He was a man of routine and with that came control. The thought of something outside of his power dictating his life made him real nervous.

Matt was quiet for a while, making Wade second guess being so honest. When he did speak, his brother was more serious than he was used to.

"Maybe it's just not worth it then? It's already a little problematic with her working for us, why complicate your life?"

What?

"I'm single Matt. I know it's been a while since you've been in the dating world, but this is what it's like…putting yourself out there, hoping that one day you'll find that one person."

Matt rolled his eyes. "You sound like some douche in a chick flick."

"What's with you, man, things okay with you and Melody?"

His brother rarely mentioned his girlfriend, despite the fact they'd been together for going on five years. They were yet to move in together though and he'd heard no talk of wedding plans.

"Yeah, of course." Matt dismissed Wade's concern with a flick of the hand. "Look, no offense, but your luck with women is bordering on fucking catastrophic."

No offense my ass. "Thanks a lot asshole."

His brother scoffed. "Come on, you've got to admit it's been a shitshow. You've been on what, three dates in two years? One didn't show up, one got carried out of the restaurant mid-date by Cody, and one ran away."

Well, when you put it like that.

"What you don't realize, man, is that you're a catch," Matt continued, ignoring Wade's snort. "I'm serious. You're a business owner, house owner, you're nice and shit, and let's face it, none of the Evans brothers have been hit with the ugly stick." A short, sharp laugh escaped him as Wade shook his head. "You just pick the wrong women."

If only it was that simple. If Wade had learned anything in his thirty-two years on this planet, it was that love had nothing to do with how good a person was on paper. He agreed with the fact that he was a decent man with plenty to offer but unfortunately the type of women he was drawn to don't care about 'good on paper guys.' Which was why he probably liked them.

"Why don't you let me set you up with one of Melody's friends. Her friend Courtney's always had a thing for you. She's a nice girl, pretty, easy…her family owns a ranch over by Splitrock."

Easy.

For the first time, Wade thought twice about his brother's relationship with Melody. Easy was a word that did come to mind. But not necessarily in a good way. Yes, when you are with the right person things should be easy. But Matt and Melody had stayed still for five years. No plans for the future. And no urgency to spend more time together. Was this really an easy relationship or just convenient?

"Thanks, but no thanks." Wade rose from the bench. "I wasn't lying when I told you I really like Riley. And for me, that's worth the risk."

Matt stood too. Scepticism clear on his face. "Okay, brother. It's your life. Just be careful, okay?"

Wade didn't reply, he didn't need to. Matt was slapping his back one minute and swaggering down to the river the next.

"Good talk," Wade mumbled to himself.

Maybe his brother wasn't the best person to open up to after all.

***

Later that day, Wade found himself up at the main house. His Ma had tempted him with freshly baked cherry pie, and he was helpless to resist. Just as he was about to help himself to a second piece, a loud crash had his knife stopping mid-slice.

Heading in the direction of the sound, it wasn't long before he heard some rather choice cursing.

"Did you just say fudge nuggets?" He chuckled as he opened the door to the laundry room. "Oh, shit, are you okay?"

As soon as he'd caught sight of Riley splayed across the vinyl floor, he was kneeling down and offering her his hand.

"No! The flipping ironing board came at me."

"It *came at you*?" He managed to fight back a smile. Just.

Riley accepted his hand and they both came to a stand. "Ow, ow, ow." She hopped. "My ankle!" Wade was picking her up seconds later and striding toward the living room. "Whoa, what are you doing, where are you taking me?"

He didn't answer, not until he'd placed her down safely onto his mother's floral couch. "Let me take a look." After dropping to his knees, he went about inspecting said ankle. Ignoring his body pulse as his fingers drifted over silky skin.

"I'm fine, really. I just need to walk it off." Riley attempted to push herself off the pink rose cushions, but Wade ushered her back down.

"Nope. Everyone knows you shouldn't put weight on an injury. You need to rest it. Maybe put some ice on it."

She looked at him like he was crazy. "I need to finish the laundry."

"I'll finish the laundry," he declared.

"*You'll* finish the laundry?" She didn't seem convinced.

"Sure will, darlin'. You're looking at a modern man right here. Cooking, cleaning, ironing, you name it—I can do it."

That dangerous smile of hers hit him full force in the stomach. "Is that so?"

"Sure is."

Their eyes locked and all he could think about was kissing her again.

Time and a place, Wade.

Right. And this wasn't it. She needed rest and ice. He'd just have to settle for cradling her in his arms again. Which is what he did next. With one rather smooth scoop, she was back in his hold. This time, he was taking her home.

CHAPTER SEVEN

Who the hell gets injured doing laundry?

Riley does apparently.

Stupid fricking ironing board.

Now here she was in Wade's big, strong arms, being carried home like a child. Every ranch hand they passed on the way to her trailer was stifling a snigger. This was humiliating. Even for her. And definitely not how she imagined their first encounter would go after their date.

"My ankle is fine. Really. I can walk." This must have been the fifth time she'd told him this, but her protest was falling on deaf ears.

"You just like hopping for the hell of it, right?" Wade's face turned to her then, blinding her with white teeth and dimples. As if she wasn't already drunk on his cologne, this was the last thing she needed.

She was quiet. Staring into deep blue. Her mouth getting dryer and dryer by the second. Evidently, it wasn't the smartest route to take. Her staring at him, caused him to stop in his tracks.

"You okay, petal?"

She wasn't, which is probably why a "no" slipped from her lips.

"Can I ask why?" He looked more amused than concerned.

"People are laughing."

"Who's laughing?" He grinned.

Well, he was for a start. "Davey and Robert."

"They weren't laughing, darlin'. I can promise you that."

She wanted to ask how he could promise her that, but she refrained. It would only prolong whatever this was. She needed him to move and get her home, so she could hide under her blanket for the rest of the evening.

"Let's uh, let's just…" There were so many things she could have said like, let's go, carry on, walk, but no. Instead, God knows why, she said, "Giddy-up."

This is why the facepalm emoji exists.

Okay, now he was laughing. And not hiding it.

"Yes, ma'am," he said in between laughs.

It was the best response she could hope for, that and the fact he'd started moving again. Now all she had to do was not die of embarrassment until they got back to her trailer.

The morning had started off so well. She was still basking in last night's kiss, the sun was out, and she was having an easy day at work. Until she wasn't.

Thankfully, Wade's long legs got them back quicker than she could even walk. But once he'd placed her on her couch, he didn't leave like a good guest should. Instead, he bagged up ice, put a pot of coffee on and went about making her a snack.

"Are you seriously making a grilled cheese right now?" She twisted to get a good look at him.

Wade didn't look up as he flipped the sandwich. "You need to eat."

"Says who?"

"Says me. You need to keep your strength up."

She could feel her face contort into a *what the fuck* expression. "For an ankle injury?"

"Yup." He was already plating up. "That and you need to rest, which means not putting unnecessary weight on it. Making your own food would put unnecessary weight on it."

Riley rolled her eyes. "Okay, Doctor Wade."

She didn't even know why she was being so salty. She loved grilled cheese. It just felt weird. She didn't understand why he was here. Looking after her.

Maybe he's afraid you're gonna sue him for a workplace injury?

Yes. That's probably it.

After placing her plate on the coffee table, Wade took a seat in the armchair next to her, his own mug of coffee in hand.

So, I guess he's not leaving.

She started to squirm. Why wasn't he leaving? Or saying anything.

Say something. It's so quiet.

"Uh…" *An actual sentence, Riley.* "Um. So. Um. I'm not going to sue you."

Coffee sprayed from Wade's mouth, followed by a short sharp laugh. "What?"

Riley realized her mistake immediately. That was a random thing to say. She really needed to stop blurting out everything that came into her head. It just always felt so much harder than it should be.

"Sorry," she rushed out. "I was thinking about that earlier, so it was on my mind, and that's why…just forget I said that please. Thank you for the grilled cheese."

"You were thinking about suing me earlier?" That didn't sound like forgetting to her.

Riley sighed. "Yeah. I was wondering why you were being so nice to me. Carrying me home. Getting me ice. Coffee. Sandwiches. Then I thought that maybe you were worried that I'd sue you. Like those accident at work ads you see. And maybe that was why you were doing all this stuff. So, I just wanted you to know that I'm not gonna sue you."

She needed to stop talking. *Food will make you stop.* Quickly leaning forward, she grabbed her plate and her grilled cheese and got to work stuffing her mouth. Expertly avoiding Wade's big blue eyes which were now penetrating her skin.

"You think that's why I'm here?"

She didn't answer. Her mouth was full of cheese. But she did meet his gaze, which was enough apparently for him to continue.

"Riley, I like you. Did I not make that clear enough last night?"

Riley gulped. Even though she'd already swallowed her sandwich.

Wade rose from the chair, his mug going to the table as he leaned into her. It all happened so quickly. One minute she was gulping, the next, stubble was grazing her chin and firm lips were awakening every nerve ending.

This was not how Riley thought their next kiss would go. Ice on her ankle, plate balancing on her lap, hands in her hair angling her head.

It was over too soon, but that didn't stop them both panting as Wade drew back. Damn. Was it normal to feel so flushed after a kiss? She was surprised her glasses hadn't steamed up. Her insides felt like they were on fire. This couldn't be healthy.

"Do you get why I'm here now?" Wade was still bent over, giving her a look so smouldering it should be illegal.

"'Cause you like me and want to kiss me?"

Her reply was met with a blinding smile, which helped to dispel some of the sexual tension making it hard to breathe.

"Yeah, petal. 'Cause I like you and want to kiss you." He repeated her words back to her. Causing her own smile to bloom.

She lost his eyes for a moment as he straightened. "Now we've cleared that up. I'm gonna head out. I've got some laundry to do."

Just minutes ago she'd wanted him to leave, so it didn't make sense that she felt disappointed, yet she did. She wanted more of those kisses. More of the burn. But of course she didn't say that. For once, she was well aware that this particular thought shouldn't leave her mouth.

"Do you need anything else before I go?" Riley shook her head. Wade paused for a moment before continuing. "I think maybe you should do the laundry at my place from now on, there's more space, so there's less chance the ironing board is gonna *come at you*."

"At your place?"

"At my place." He nodded. "Don't worry, they'll be no funny business. We'll keep everything strictly professional."

He's talking about sex, right?

"What if I want funny business?" she asked seriously.

"I'm not opposed to funny business," he said with a smirk. "As long as it's outside work hours."

"Technically, it's work hours now..." *And you just kissed me.*

Wade chuckled. "That it is, petal. That it is. Tomorrow is your day off though, right? How 'bout I come take care of you?"

"Don't you have to work?"

Wade shrugged. "Perks of being the boss. So...is that a yes?"

Riley didn't need to check her poor excuse for a social calendar to know that she was free. Other than plans with Bella on Friday night, her week consisted of work and hibernation. But she suddenly felt nervous. What if Wade wanted to have funny business tomorrow?

You don't know what funny business is!

True. She didn't. But the twinkle in his eye when he'd said it had told her everything she needed to know.

"What's wrong?"

Right. *You answer questions out loud, Riley.* "Uh. Nothing. Tomorrow is fine with me."

Note to self, google "funny business."

***

The combination of ice and sitting on her ass for four

hours obviously did something because later that night, Riley's ankle felt back to normal. It made her feel guilty. All that fuss and she was fine. What was she supposed to do when Wade showed up tomorrow to look after her?

Fake it?

She couldn't do that. Could she?

While pondering her moral quandary, her phone began to light up. Followed shortly by upbeat chimes filling her small space. She knew who it was before she'd even got a glimpse at the name. It was the same person who called her every night. Her mom.

Swiping right, she was quick to give her mother her cheeriest hello.

"Where were you last night?" *Here we go. Getting straight to it then.*

"Oh, yeah, I had an early night, I wasn't feeling well."

"What's wrong?" her mom was quick to ask. "Are you okay? Do you have a temperature? Have you been to the doctor?"

Why did she have to go and say she wasn't well? She should know better. "I'm fine. I was just a little tired that's all. I feel better now. Please don't worry about me."

"Hank! Hank!" *Oh, God.* "Riley's sick!"

Riley slumped back into the cushions and resisted the urge to roll her eyes. She knew her parents meant well. It was natural to worry.

This much?

No. Not this much. But they hadn't always been like this. They'd gone from relaxed, carefree, normal people to intense and overbearing in the blink of an eye. It all started when Riley was eleven. When her cousin disappeared. It didn't matter that they found Violet three days later, shacked up with her boyfriend. Those three days were enough to scare the living daylights out of her parents. From then on, they had to know where she was and who she was with at all times. Even now. It's why Riley had to leave. She needed to be free.

"Are you still there?" Her mother's panicked voice brought her back to the present.

"Yes, Mom, I'm still here."

The rest of the conversation consisted mostly of Riley reassuring her parents that she was okay. It was the one conversation she'd mastered over the years. Because she had to.

ISOBEL REED

CHAPTER EIGHT

Wade had been in Riley's trailer for the grand total of sixty seconds, which was a brand-new record for the time it had taken for him to be rendered speechless. He liked to think of himself as prepared for most situations' life had a habit of throwing at him, but this one, this one he felt utterly unprepared for.

"Run that by me again, darlin'?" He took in a sharp breath.

"Um. Yes. Okay." Riley nodded, a look of sheer determination sparkling in those big brown eyes. "I said, my ankle is much better. So I think we should have sex."

Yeah. That's what I thought she said.

The confirmation didn't help him wrangle up a response though. Leaving her words dangling in the now even thicker air.

"What?" Riley's head tilted with the question. "Why does your face look like that?"

God knows what his face was doing but if it was anything like the internal battle going on between his head and his dick, then she was in for a right show.

"You don't want to have sex?" Riley guessed.

Time to use your words, Wade.

He cleared his throat. Slowly. And attempted to fix his face as he wondered how best to break the news that it was official, his head had won the battle.

"Riley, petal, trust me when I tell you that you have no idea just how much I want to have sex with you." *Dial it back a little maybe? You're coming off desperate.* "But don't you think it's a little early?"

He watched closely as Riley's hand dropped to cradle her wrist. She was thumbing her pulse point again.

Shit. That can't be good.

Wade gave her a moment. Waiting anxiously for her to gather her thoughts, already regretting not immediately stripping her naked and bending her over the couch.

Finally, she spoke. "How long do you usually wait to have sex?"

He was struck by the lack of emotion behind the question. She didn't look offended like he worried she might. Or pissed. She wanted facts.

"Uh, well, I've never really put a timeline on it before, darlin'. It normally just happens when it feels right."

If he was really honest, he couldn't actually remember. It had been so damn long since he last had sex that he wouldn't be surprised if he'd forgotten what to do.

You're a real fucking catch.

"On average, how many dates did it take to feel right?"

"I don't know." She was really putting him on the spot now. "Three or four maybe."

Riley nodded. "Isn't this our third date?" Before he had a chance to reply, she continued. "I guess it depends on if you count the wedding or when we went to Goldacre."

She really wants to have sex with you, man. Just have sex with her. Drop the gentleman act for one day for God's sake.

The problem was it wasn't an act. It was who he was. And as much as he wanted to take the beautiful woman standing before him, he knew that it was too soon.

"The other night, at my house, let's count that as our first official date. Which means I need to take you out at least two more times before we…" he deliberately trailed off. "I hadn't planned on doing that today but seeing as your ankle's better, we should do something. So, what do you think, are you up for date number two right now?"

A small smile tipped her lips up. "Okay."

"Okay." he agreed. Capturing her hand he led her toward the trailer door.

"Wait." Riley tugged him to a halt; he was quick to twist and get a look at the concern creasing her brow. "So our next date, after today, we'll have sex after that?"

Jesus Christ. She was killing him.

Wade swallowed hard and ignored the twinge in his pants. Like a gentleman.

"If that's what you want, petal." Was the only thing he managed to come up with.

"It is." She nodded again. "Okay. Let's go. Giddy up." The smile she gave him this time was blinding.

She was too tempting to resist, and he didn't want to anymore. There was only so much self-control he was capable of. So he dipped his head. And within seconds, had seized her lips. Nipping, sucking and feasting on all the sweet moans he was able to drag out of her.

Sweet Jesus.

He knew he needed to pull back. Before he changed his mind. With every swipe of his tongue, he was remembering exactly what to do. He hadn't forgotten. It was all coming back to him.

Reluctantly, after capturing one last whimper, he drew back slowly. Admiring his handiwork as he revelled in glazed eyes and an abused, wet red pout.

Perfection.

"We should get out of here, darlin'." The words were scraped from his throat. He needed out of there. Now. Luckily, he knew just the place. "Come on." Taking Riley's hand, he led them out of the trailer, into the crisp fall air.

"Where are we going?" she asked, easily matching his large strides down the pebble path.

Pausing mid-step, he turned to her then. "We're going trout fishing." He smiled. "Rumor has it, you make a mean smoked trout."

"Really?" she beamed.

"Really."

Goddamnit. The way she was looking at him, did something to him. Something dangerous.

***

Two hours later, Wade was back to square one. Staring temptation right in the face. Trout in tow, they'd headed back to his house to cook. He hadn't thought this through. This was a bad idea.

His eyes darted to Riley's ass once again as she bent down to pick up the spoon she'd just dropped.

Yeah. This is a bad idea.

Wade had spent most of their fishing trip regretting not taking Riley up on her offer. And now the universe was taunting him. Laughing in his face. He should have known this was how the day was going to go when they'd reached the river earlier. Within minutes of arriving, she'd set up her rod and caught her first fish. And damn if that didn't turn him on.

So now you have an angler fetish?

No. He was sure he didn't. Pretty sure. That would be weird.

Focus!

Right.

Fuck it.

Wade stalked to the kitchen counter where Riley was unloading their catch and wasted no time spinning her around to face him. Then he swooped. Not even waiting for her to find her balance. He'd waited long enough.

His mouth finally back on hers, he was ready to change his mind. Screw being a gentleman, he wanted her. So fucking bad.

As he pulled her closer, both his hands slipped down. One going straight to her hip while the other moved slower, his knuckles pausing over the pounding of her heart before lightly brushing the curve of her breast. Matching her whimpers with his own groan, he took the kiss deeper. She tasted like goddamn heaven.

Another swipe of his tongue and he felt her nipple harden beneath his fingers. Jesus. He was groaning again. Or was that a growl?

Who the hell cares?

He certainly didn't. He was embracing the beast she brought out in him. That was made clear when he released her lips only to sink his teeth into the crook of her neck seconds later. He teased, then licked, and teased again. Delighting as Riley dropped her head back and let out a sexy mew.

"I want you," he whispered against her skin.

Sacrificing the feel of her soft body for a moment, he lifted her onto the countertop.

"Spread your legs," he demanded. To which she immediately complied.

He liked that. And not just because she'd done what he'd wanted. But because of the fire he'd seen in her eyes when he'd asked.

Stepping between jean clad thighs, he decided to push further.

"Hands above your head." His voice sounded just as dirty as his thoughts. And as he watched Riley lift her arms, they only got dirtier.

Pushing his fingers under her top, he kept his eyes locked on hers as he slowly lifted the flimsy material. His blood heating more and more with every heavy breath she took.

It didn't take long for the top to hit the floor while Wade took in the beautiful sight before him. Silk curves wrapped in pink lace.

Riley's arms were still up. Goddamn. If he didn't know this woman was made for him before, he did now.

Going in for another taste, his kiss turned possessive as

he reached up to guide Riley's hands together. His knuckles then began their descent downward, caressing each smooth dip from her wrist to her elbow, under her arm and over the pink lace. He didn't miss her quiver beneath his touch. Or the growing impatience of her whimpers.

He wanted to see more. Touch it all. Taste everything.

His hands went to the button on her jeans, within seconds they were open, her zip pulled down and his fingers in her panties.

Fuck me.

It was his turn to groan again as he got his first feel of what was waiting for him. She was soaked. Enough for him to want to beat his chest. But as his fingers began to dip further inside, he felt her tense up. That's when he lost her lips.

"I-I, umm, I-I can't," she spluttered between pants. "I think you're right. We, uh, we should wait…until our third date."

Wade managed to swallow down his latest groan as his hand slipped from between her thighs. He chose to ignore the panic in her voice and not focus on the "can't" part of her speech. It was a lady's prerogative to change her mind. He would always respect that.

But he needed a moment to get himself together. He chose to take it while bending down to grab Riley's top.

Fuck.

Damnit, he was so turned on it was hard to form a sentence. But he had to. He knew that as soon as he heard the word "sorry" slip from Riley's perfect pink lips.

After handing her the shirt, he softly ran his thumb across her lower lip. "Petal, don't ever be sorry for telling me what you want."

"But…" she breathed. "Aren't you," her eyes darted to his crotch. "Don't you need to…"

What?

"Riley, I'm perfectly capable of controlling myself." He chanced a smile. "Like I said earlier, we can wait until it feels right—until you feel comfortable. We don't have to put a date on it."

"No—" she rushed out, quickly pulling the top over her head. "I want to. Our next date. That's when I want to."

Something was going on, but he wasn't sure what. It was like she was in a hurry, to dare he say it, "get it over with". Yet, here he was giving in to temptation and she wanted to wait. Talk about a head fuck.

"Is that okay?" The uncertainty cracking her voice snapped him back to reality. "I mean, you still want to?"

"I still want to." He was quick to confirm, taking a step back, allowing her to jump down from the counter.

Now that they'd come to some sort of understanding, he expected them to continue with their date. Smoke some trout, drink some juice, and relax. But Riley had other ideas. She was running again. She hadn't even said anything yet, but Wade could see it coming a mile away. She was eyeing the nearest exit.

Seeing as he was well in need of a cold ass shower, he decided to make it easy for her.

"This weekend," he announced. "I'll plan something for us to do. How does that sound?"

Riley shyly nodded.

"You want me to take you home?"

"No. I-I…"

"Okay," he cut her off. He wasn't going to push her, not unless it was dark out. And she didn't need to explain. Taking a step toward her, he dipped down and lay a kiss on her forehead. "I'll see you Saturday, petal."

And then she was gone.

CHAPTER NINE

"So…you ran?" Bella was smiling again as she crossed her arms and fell back into the leather cushioned couch.

Did she not just hear what Riley had said?

Maybe you should say it again.

Yes. Maybe she'd jumbled her words again.

"We were about to have sex. My top was off. And I-I just froze. And, and, his hand was down…"

"So, you ran?" Bella repeated.

Technically she had ran. Again. And Wade let her. Made it easy even. Wait. Was that a bad thing? Was there a chance he'd changed his mind?

"Hold on," Bella said as she shook her head. "Where did he have his hand?"

"Whose hand was where?" Luke's booming voice was in the room before the man himself. And he was shortly followed in by another man.

This was exactly what Riley was afraid of when she agreed to come over for drinks. More awkward social interactions. *So much for girls' night.* It wasn't Bella's fault though. Riley should've known this would happen. When she'd met Luke at the Evans wedding, it was damn clear the man couldn't stay away from his girlfriend for long. And here he was. With a friend.

A hot friend.

Yes. Hot. Which meant she'd likely act even more stupid than usual. Great. What was going on with the men in Woodvalley? Was there something in the water here? Why was everyone so good-looking?

"Well hello there." The hot friend grinned, before bumping Luke's elbow. "Luke…you going to introduce me to your beautiful guest?"

Suddenly her cheeks set on fire. There was no doubt she was red. Bright red.

Luke simply sighed. "Riley, I apologise in advance—"

"Hey!" The other man smacked Luke's arm. Hard.

"Ow. Okay. Fine. Riley, this is Benny. Benny, this is Riley."

Bella was next to speak. "Benny works with Luke, he's a firefighter too." *Of course he is.*

Why the women of Woodvalley didn't spend their days just lighting fires, she didn't know. Even she was tempted.

Riley didn't say anything. It was better that way. She simply nodded and internally begged her face to cool the hell down.

"It's nice to meet you, Riley." Benny sauntered over and extended his hand.

Does he want me to shake it?

In her panic, she extended her hand too. But she didn't shake his hand. Because it was the wrong one. Two right hands don't shake. Something she realized mid-lift. So there her hand hovered. Looking limp. And directionless.

Oh my God. I hate myself.

Benny didn't seem phased, he took her hand and brought it up to his lips, placing a soft kiss on her skin.

"May I?" he asked, nodding to the cushion next to her.

May he what?

She looked to Bella for help.

"Back off Benny, she's taken," Bella announced.

Oh. That wasn't the kind of help she'd been seeking. If anything, she felt more uncomfortable now.

"Well, that's a darn shame." Benny was still smiling.

Abnormally wide. "Who's the lucky guy?"

"It's Wade's woman," Luke announced.

Wade's woman.

Was it wrong that she kind of liked that?

"Lucky guy." Benny flashed that charming smile back her way. "He swooped in quick I'm guessing. I mean, you're new to Woodvalley, right?"

How did he know she was new in town? Surely Woodvalley Pines wasn't so small that everyone knew each other?

Bella's snort pulled her from her thoughts. "Benny here knows all the females in town. *Intimately.*"

Riley watched on as Benny rolled his eyes at Bella's comment. "Don't listen to her, darlin', she's new in town too."

Another snort emitted from her friend. "I'm not that new! And I've been here long enough to know you're the town bike."

Town bike?

Riley was so curious, she broke her comfortable silence to ask, "You've had a lot of girlfriends?"

Both Luke and Bella sniggered as Benny attempted to give them both a stern look.

"I wouldn't use the word *girlfriends* exactly, more like—"

"One-night stands?" Bella chimed.

Oh. Riley understood now. He was a player. She finally got the whole bike reference. *Clever.*

"You realize that your boyfriend wasn't exactly a choir boy either?" Benny was quick to shoot back.

"Okay, okay." Luke's hands went up. "Let's all calm down, we're all friends here. Bella is well aware of my past, and Benny, you just haven't found the right woman yet, right?"

"Exactly." Benny turned his attention back to Riley, sporting his mischievous grin. "You sure you don't want to ditch Wade and try me out instead—you could be the one I've been waiting for?"

Riley didn't know what to say to that. She wasn't used to men showing interest in her. And she definitely wasn't used to all eyes being on her. Expectantly. Her palms were beginning to sweat as panic set in.

What do I say? They're waiting for me to say something. Think of something.

"You've, uh, you've never…um, you've never had a girlfriend?"

She did it. She segued successfully. Like a goddamn conversation master. And she was feeling extremely pleased with herself, until she caught a look at Benny. His cheeky smile had been wiped clean off his boyish face.

Said the wrong thing again. Idiot.

"Um, sorry," Riley started but then stopped. She couldn't think of what else to say.

Luckily for her, Benny was quick to replace his frown with a shiny new smile. A less genuine one. "No need to be sorry, darlin'. Of course I've had a girlfriend before."

"Since when?" Luke heckled.

"Not all of us are emotionally stunted, Cappelli," Benny shot back at his friend, before turning to Riley. "We all had a high school sweetheart, right?" *No.* "Well, I did too." He shrugged. "Together all through high school, even made it for a year after, too."

"What happened?" Riley and Bella asked at the same time.

"Same thing that happens to every high school relationship…it ended." He laughed, rather unconvincingly.

Riley may not be the best at reading people, or be good at anything remotely related to socialising, but even she could see the sadness radiating off this man. There was a story there. One he clearly didn't want to talk about.

Bella rose from her seat and grabbed Riley's hand. "Okay. We're going." Riley was up now, too and being dragged out of the room. "We'll be upstairs if you need us. You boys have fun."

And upstairs they went, straight into Bella and Luke's

bedroom, where her new friend gestured for her to take a seat on the bed. The décor was much more masculine than she was expecting. She watched Bella rummaging in the fitted wooden wardrobe.

A paper bag was placed in front of Riley a moment later. "So, I went shopping in Goldacre the other day and I got you something," Bella said. Looking apprehensive. "It's lingerie. For your date."

"Lingerie?" Riley was so confused.

"Yeah. For you, not for him."

Okay. Now she was even more confused. "What?"

"You know, to make you feel more confident. You'd be amazed what wearing sexy underwear can do for your confidence." Bella pushed the bag at her, urging her to open it.

"Other than me, my mom is the only person who has ever bought me underwear."

"Well, I doubt you or your mom have bought this kind of underwear." She giggled as Riley pulled the lacy material from the bag.

She stared. Her fingers going to the waistband of the panties and pulling them wide. Her gaze then dropped to the tag. And the price.

"You paid thirty dollars for this?"

Bella quickly snagged the tag. "Ignore the price. So? What do you think?"

"I think you need to get your money back; there's a string where the material is supposed to be."

Laughter filled the room. But only until Bella realized Riley wasn't joking.

"It's a g-string, honey. Tell me you've heard of a g-string."

She'd heard of one. Seen them. And actively avoided them. The idea of a string up her ass wasn't very appealing to her. Which is exactly what she told her friend.

"You don't have to wear it," Bella reassured her. "I just thought it might help booster your confidence on your date.

Make you feel sexy. It's always helped me. Way before I even met Luke, if I was having a bad day or feeling low, I used to treat myself to new lingerie. It didn't matter that no one but me would see it, it made me feel good about myself."

Riley looked at the red material again. In a new light. If she was going to have sex with Wade on their next date, she would need some of that confidence Bella was talking about.

Let's face it, you need all the help you can get.

That was true. She did. Even if it came in the form of a string up her butt.

***

It was Saturday night. Date night. And the night Riley would finally lose her virginity.

"I think I'm gonna hurl," Riley muttered to herself as she high tailed it to the bathroom.

No. False alarm.

Thank God. The last thing she needed was to get sick and ruin the results of two hours' worth of preening and plucking. But she still felt nauseous. Very, very nauseous. No matter how ready she was to finally go to bed with someone, it didn't make it any less terrifying.

Two bangs on the trailer door caused her to jump. Wade was here.

Pulling herself up from the cold tile, she quickly checked her face in the mirror before scurrying through the living room.

"Hi," she squeaked as she swung open the door.

"Petal." Wade used his index finger to nudge up his cream Stetson. "Looking beautiful as always, darlin'."

Riley nodded. Not in agreement, just because she didn't know what else to do. Or say. So nodding it was.

Why are you still doing it, though?

Okay. It was a long nod. One that she stopped abruptly.

"Shall we?" Wade's hand was out, waiting for hers.

More nodding ensued as she took his hand and was led outside. As usual, he didn't push for conversation as he ushered her inside his truck and rounded the front. Even as they drove through the ranch's dirt roads their silence remained comfortable.

When they finally pulled to a stop, Wade spoke. "So, I know we haven't gone far, and *technically* we are in the middle of a field." There was no technically about it. They were definitely in a field. "But I was thinking about where I could take you that was crowd free, had a good view, and that would feed you well."

"It's definitely crowd free." She smiled. "The view is...a field. And food wise...are we testing out the farm to table idea?"

Wade's deep laugh filled the cab. God. Even that was sexy. She watched on, fascinated, as dimples punctuated his grin. And bright blue eyes glistened as they caught the last of the sun. It was then she realized something. She didn't have to wait. She didn't have to spend their whole date nervous about what would happen after it. She could do this now. Then they could enjoy the rest of the evening.

Go on then.

There was the catch. If she wanted to do this—she had to initiate it.

Before she got too in her head, she leaned over and did the only thing she could think of. She kissed him. And she continued kissing him even when he gasped in shock.

It was a messy exchange, and she was sure she was doing it wrong. Clumsily. Luckily, before she knew it, Wade's shock was gone, and he was taking control. Just the way she liked it.

Big hands cradled her face as he managed to get deeper. The taste of his tongue making her brain fuzzy. And her skin feeling hotter and hotter as he thrust her back. His hard chest pushing into her soft one.

Wade drew back slowly, until choppy breaths were

moistening her lips.

"Goddamn, petal." He sighed. "You kiss me like that again, and we're not gonna make it through dinner."

"We can eat later." *Am I panting?*

This time, Wade backed up further, until he was looking into her.

Yep. I'm panting.

"That's what you want?" he asked as his gaze darkened.

It took her a moment to realize that he wasn't just talking about the food. And when she did, she was nodding again. But he didn't look convinced.

"I'm gonna need words, darlin'."

She didn't understand the concern wrinkling his brow. Or the scrape in his voice. Weren't men supposed to want this? You would think they'd jump at the chance of skipping over the formalities and getting on with the good stuff.

"That's what I want," she announced, with a lot more confidence in her voice than in her stomach.

Thankfully, her declaration seemed to be enough to satisfy him as moments later his mouth was back on hers, prying her apart as he lowered them down into the leather seat.

Riley didn't know if it was the feel of his body pressing into hers or the feral noises she was swallowing but she suddenly felt desperate. Desperate for more. Desperate for everything. She needed to feel his skin. Taste it. Get a good look at what exactly was currently pushing between her thighs and making her want to scream.

Wade's mouth was on the move. His wet lips skimming her jaw and tracing her ear. "Spread your legs," he rasped.

She obeyed immediately, her dress hitching up as she made room for his hard body. As soon as he repositioned himself her head fell back and an embarrassingly loud whimper filled the cab. And it only got louder as he bared his teeth and dragged them down her throat. Nipping. Sucking. Kissing. All while his hips did magical things.

Oh. Wow.

But as his head dipped lower, panic began to set in. Could he feel just how wet her panties had become? Was she too wet? Was that a thing? So many questions and no one to answer them. And it wouldn't look great if she pulled out her phone mid-thrust to google it.

Stop overthinking it. He's going to be inside of you for God's sake. Who cares if your panties are wet, they're not going to stay on long anyway.

Yes. True. She welcomed sensible thoughts for once. Now she could get back to moaning just in time for Wade's hand to push up her dress.

"Fuck," his hand was on her hip, his thumb leisurely stroking back and forth over the flimsy red lace as he stared down. The rise and fall of his chest becoming more labored with each breath. "On your stomach," he demanded.

Guess he wants to look at the back—or lack of it.

She did as she was told. Carefully twisting on the narrow seat until she was inhaling leather.

"Goddamn." She felt Wade's fingers trace the curve of her ass. "Did you get these especially for me, petal?"

There was something in his voice. Something dark. And it was turning her on even more. As if it were possible.

"Yes," she whispered. Letting out a sigh as he cast the tiny string aside. Baring her to him.

She was exposed. Vulnerable. And she loved every second of it.

"Is this for me, too?" She felt his fingers move lower and lower until they stroked her centre.

Well, he definitely knows how wet you are now.

'Yes," she repeated, another whimper escaping as he pushed a thick digit inside of her. "Oh God, yes."

Riley rocked into him. It was as if her body had taken over all control. Apparently, it knew what it wanted and had no problem asking for it. Another digit was pushed inside and this time, she screamed. Not in pain, but in pleasure.

Wade was either an expert at this or she'd been doing something seriously wrong when taking care of herself because nothing had felt this good before. And it was only getting better as his body was hovering over her again. Fingers still very much inside of her, his lips were on her back. Teasing her with his tongue. Sucking. Biting. Pulling noises out of her she never knew existed.

Riley faintly felt her dress being pushed even higher until it reached the nape of her neck. And her bra being unclipped.

Did he do that with one hand?

He did. But evidently, he needed another to strip her completely, which is what he did next. After sliding out of her, he gently tugged her dress up and discarded it. Her bra was the next victim and then those red panties.

I'm very fucking naked.

A fact that only hit home as a still fully dressed Wade flipped her over. The slight sting of insecurity was quick to fade though as she caught sight of the raw intensity radiating off him. He wanted her. That was pretty clear. And just when she thought she couldn't want him more, his shirt was lifted over his head and tossed to the side.

Good grief!

"You ready for me, petal?" His hands went to his belt buckle.

Yes. God, yes. Hurry up.

Another nod and Wade's knees pushed her open as he unbuttoned and unzipped. Breathing got much harder after that. Even her vision blurred as jeans and boxers were yanked down.

Wade's powerful body was pressing into her again, the heat of his skin warming her insides as he seized her lips with an urgency she hadn't felt before.

Riley's body was once again in charge. Her nails clawing Wade's muscular back, as she rolled her hips. Begging for more. Something had awoken in her. And she knew there would be no putting it back as she moaned and arched and wrapped her legs around the man making her world tilt.

Her impatient whines were getting louder as his tongue

plunged deeper and her hips rocked harder. Wade got the message. He repositioned himself and emitted a savage growl as he sunk into her.

Ow.

Clouds cleared in that moment. Her brain was back on and her eyes shot open just in time for Wade to release her lips. He hadn't moved. And when she got a look at his face, she knew why.

So much for not telling him.

Talk about a mood killer.

Just when she thought he was going to pull out and run for the hills, Wade surprised her. His wild Sex God demeanour gentled as he steadied himself above her.

"Just breathe, baby." He was reassuring her with throaty whispers. "You're in control. You tell me when to move."

"Okay," she managed through shaky breaths. "Now. I think now."

After planting a soft kiss on her lips, he drew back slowly before pushing into her again. With less force this time. Riley released a long exhale, relieved that the sting was gone. And her lust had resurfaced. That's when she kissed him again and encouraged him to move. And move he did.

Fuck me.

Literally.

CHAPTER TEN

Wade was still catching his breath. Yet the lust-fuelled fog was already starting to clear. Leaving the reality of what just happened to hit him full force in the chest.

What the actual—

She was a freaking virgin. And her first time was not only with him, but on the seat of his beat-up old truck. *Real fucking classy, man.* There should have been a bed. A bath. Goddamn rose petals. Not to mention a real date.

"Why didn't you tell me?" Wade was still hovering over her, Riley's legs holding him firmly in place.

He watched on as her mouth opened to speak but nothing came out.

"You should have told me," he continued.

"What would have happened if I had told you?" she whispered. "Would we still have had sex in your truck?"

Hell no, we wouldn't have.

"Darlin'…"

"Exactly," she cut him off. "I wanted to have sex in your truck." The hold she'd had around his waist eased as she untangled herself.

Lifting himself up, he couldn't help but smile. This woman was something else.

How has she not had sex before?

Wade studied her as her head lifted and she propped

herself up on her elbows. God she was beautiful.

"This should have happened in a bed, petal."

"Why?" Riley's head tilted with the question.

"So you're comfortable, so I can take care of you, before and after."

Wade was no expert, but he was pretty damn sure most women didn't envision their first time in the cab of a pick-up truck.

"Take care of me...how?"

This conversation wasn't going the way he thought it would. But then again, it never did when it came to Riley.

It didn't escape his notice that they were both still very naked. Wade on his knees between Riley's wide-open thighs. Running his eyes down her hot body, he stopped at her centre. Which was where his hand gravitated.

Using his thumb, he brushed back and forth, letting wetness seep into his skin. "Are you sore?"

"A little." His eyes shot back up just in time to see her bite down on her lower lip.

This is where a bath would have come in useful.

"If I'd have known..." He moved his hand until he was cupping her, his fingers sliding under her ass as his thumb continued to stroke. "I'd have spent longer getting you ready for me." Riley's breathing hitched. "You needed my mouth...my tongue." He felt her squirm beneath his touch, his thumb starting to soak. "Would you have liked that, petal? My head between these thighs?"

Yes, he was teasing her now. But he couldn't help himself. She brought out something in him. A dominant side, he'd never explored before. And it was clear she liked it just as much as he did.

She rocked into his hand, reminding him it wasn't too late to soothe her. Some after care which would make them both feel good.

There wasn't enough room for him to lie down, so he needed to improvise. Reluctantly, he stopped stroking and used both his hands to lift Riley's legs until they were folded over his shoulders. Ignoring her gasp, he felt himself smile as he got his first taste. And it only got bigger as he felt her body shake and her moan vibrate down his throat.

Fucking heaven.

***

Wade squinted at the light filtering through his bedroom curtains. *What time is it?* And why wasn't his alarm blaring?

He was still blinking as he pushed himself up from the mattress. That's when he noticed Riley, tiptoeing around his bedroom in last night's dress.

"Looking for something, darlin'?" he croaked, his voice evidently yet to wake up.

The sheepish smile she gave him was worth opening his eyes for. "Um, I may have, um, misplaced my panties."

He was officially awake. And grinning. She was at the side of the bed now, rubbing her wrist. And he couldn't resist tugging her back inside. This was their morning after, and he wanted to enjoy every second of it.

"You don't need panties in here." He gently pulled her into him, wrapping his arms around her as she laughed softly. "In fact, let's just call this a no panties zone."

More musical giggles filled the room. "I've got to work," she half-heartedly protested as she snuggled into his chest. "My boss is a real stickler for time management."

It was his turn to laugh. "Is that so?" He held her tighter, his chin sinking into silky hair. "Tell me more about this boss of yours."

Riley's head poked up until molten brown eyes held him hostage. "What do you want to know?"

"Oh, you know, the usual. Is he handsome? Good in bed?"

Her mouth dropped open, and a smack landed on his bare chest. "Wade!" she squeaked. "I thought you said there'd be no funny business at work?"

"Last time I checked, petal, we weren't at work." He

placed a soft kiss on her forehead. "Also...I don't believe there's any funny business happening presently. But I'd be happy to change that."

"I have work...so do you!" That wasn't a no.

Twisting until Riley was on her back, Wade positioned himself above her, a teasing smile on his lips. "I promise to talk to your boss if you're late."

He didn't miss her eyes twinkle or her teeth digging into her lower lip. And he definitely didn't miss the flush creeping up her neck. She wanted him, just as much as he wanted her. Again.

Letting his forehead brush hers, he dropped the playful act, his voice just as serious as his request. "Stay?"

"Okay," she whispered.

Claiming her lips, he took his time savoring the softness. Getting high on the familiar sting of citrus. The wetter the kiss got, the more whimpers he swallowed. It was addictive.

When he eventually pulled back, they were both panting. Hooded eyes making his body pulsate.

"Tell me what you want. What you like." His voice deepened.

She hesitated. Looking unsure. So he asked again. "Tell me." Or more like demanded.

"I...I..." He felt her shake. Not with nerves though. Something else. There was something she wanted. He just needed to get what it was out of her.

"Whatever it is, darlin', I'll give it to you," he reassured.

She gulped. And nodded. "I-I, um, I like it...I like it when you tell me what to do." Wade felt his jaw tick and nostrils flare as his breathing picked up. "It means I don't have to think," she continued. "I can just feel. And enjoy."

When she was done, she nodded a second time. Looking proud of herself. And a little shocked.

This woman was made for him. It wasn't a coincidence she brought out a side of him he'd never fully explored. It was her. She was who he was meant to explore it with.

"I like that too," he admitted. "I really fucking like it."

Riley looked relieved. Turned on. And sexy as hell as her tongue ran over her lips.

"Lose the dress," he ordered, going to his knees to give her space to do so. Growing harder by the second as she scrambled up to do what she was told. "And the bra."

Once she was completely naked, she looked to him, expectantly. Waiting to hear his next demand. He was damn happy to oblige.

"On your back. Legs open." Again, she complied, her hips rolling as she put herself on full display.

God-fucking-damn.

The things he wanted to do to her. Would do. Just thinking about it was making him throb.

Now they weren't in his truck, he could take his time. Run his mouth over every inch of her. Learn what makes her scream, beg, and shake.

What are you waiting for?

Spoilt for choice, he didn't know where to start.

"Please," Riley breathed, surprising him with the blatant want. So blatant, she was writhing in his sheets.

Decision made, he leaned forward, his mouth going to her thick, luscious thighs. Just a taste, long enough to let his warm breath sink into her. Teasing her. Before his nose nudged upward. His tongue darting out, desperate to lap up salty citrus.

A growl emitted from him as Riley arched, throwing her head back as labored pants made the air hum. Anticipation coating his lips as he neared her centre.

When he got there, the patience he assumed he'd have was nowhere to be found. He wanted her. In his mouth. On his fingers. Dripping down his thighs.

So he took it.

CHAPTER ELEVEN

Day two of not being a virgin and Riley felt like a new woman. A more confident one. A happier one—*thank you multiple orgasms*. And a stronger one. Which would explain why she agreed to a girl's lunch today at The Tipsy Cow. With not just Bella, but with a woman called Cat and another woman called Rachel.

You've got this.

Okay. As free as she felt, she was still her, and still nervous. That was clear to anyone who bothered to look her way as her leg tapped up and down on the wooden floor.

Riley was early and had scoped out a booth in the dark corner of the local tavern. Away from the dance floor and away from the older cowboys perched on stools along the bar. Here she could sip on her orange juice, stare at the odd neon signs scattered all over the walls and freak out in peace.

"Hi." Riley's head lifted at Bella's cheery voice. Immediately, she noticed that her new friend wasn't alone.

Offering a nervous smile to each of the women as they approached the table, it was the tall, slender woman with long black hair that spoke first.

"Hi, Riley! I think we briefly met at Libby's wedding, but we didn't get a chance to chat." She slid into the booth opposite her. "I'm Cat." *Is that a British accent?*

Before Riley could reply, the petite redhead was sliding

into the seat next to her. "And I'm Rachel, nice to meet you, sugar." A kind smile was flashed her way.

Bella had taken a seat next to Cat. And they were now all looking at Riley. Expectantly.

Now would be a good time to talk.

"Um, hi," she mumbled. "Um, Bella has told me a lot about you."

"Same," Cat replied, a mischievous glint in her piercing blue eyes. "I think her exact words were... 'Riley's awesome'. She's also warned us to be on our best behaviour too, in case we scare you off, so she must *really* like you."

Scare me off?

"Actually," Bella interrupted, "what I said was—maybe wait until your third lunch with her to start with the sex jokes."

Cat rolled her eyes in response before turning to Bella. "You all act like I'm some kind of sex pest. I'm a respectable woman I'll have you know. A mum and everything."

"Talking of which, I heard you got into it with Betty-Jo the other day at the school gate?" Rachel inquired.

Cat shrugged. "Yeah, well, Betty-Jo's son has been bothering Dylan, so it was just a friendly reminder that if her son continued to be a dick, then I had no trouble being one too." A sly grin spread across her face.

"I don't think you can call a ten-year-old a *dick*," Rachel chastised while Bella giggled.

Cat treated Rachel to another shrug. "Being a *dick* isn't restricted to age, honey. Some people are just born that way."

Bella was laughing harder now. And louder. Riley couldn't help but smile. These women were funny. The more they talked around her, the more her nerves were easing.

"Right." Cat's hands came down on the dark wood table. "I'm getting drinks. Shall I order us some food too? I was thinking burger and fries all round unless anyone has any objections?"

There was a resounding "yes please" from Rachel and Bella. Eyes turned to her again afterward, where she choked out a "um, yes, fine with me." That was all it took for Cat to disappear over to the bar.

Bella and Rachel chatted amongst themselves after that and seemed satisfied with a few head nods for answers when they tried to include Riley. She was working her way up to a conversation. Or at least that's what she kept telling herself.

Once Cat returned, talk turned to their friend Libby. She learned all about how Libby and Zach would be taking their honeymoon in Europe next spring. How Cat and Rachel thought they were trying for a baby. And what amazing aunts they would all be.

"Oh my God." Rachel's hand covered Riley's arm. "I just had a thought. If you marry Wade, you and Libby will be sisters-in-law."

Um...what was that now?

"Don't worry," Cat interjected, "Libby's the nice one. She'd be an excellent sister-in-law."

"Um, excuse me! What about me?" Rachel squeaked. Clearly offended.

"Oh, yeah, sorry." Cat laughed. "Correction—Libby *and Rachel* are the nice ones."

It was Bella's turn to be offended. "I resent that. I'm nice!"

"You're okay."

Bella's gaze swung to Riley. From Bella's reaction, she guessed that she was doing a bad job of hiding her horror.

"Guys. Enough," Bella ordered. "This is what I'm talking about. What happened to not scaring her off?"

Rachel and Cat exchanged guilty expressions before turning to Riley.

"Sorry," they both said at the same time. "Don't run," Rachel sweetly pleaded.

"Yeah, please don't. We'll never hear the end of it if you do." Cat's comment was met with an arm smack from Bella. "Ow!"

"Why don't you tell us a little more about yourself, sugar," Rachel continued. "How are you liking working on the Evans ranch?"

All eyes were back on her. She hated that. It was too much pressure. And her thoughts were spiralling. They all knew about her and Wade. How?

Oh no. What if Bella told them about me being a virgin?

Surely not. Bella didn't seem like the gossipy type. But then again, she hadn't known her long enough to completely rule it out.

"I'd say it's going damn well personally; she's bagged herself a hot cowboy," Cat chimed in. "Ow." And received another smack.

"Uh, it's good," Riley mumbled. "I'm good at cleaning."

She mentally sighed at her own response. All that small talk practice and that's all she could come up with. *I'm good at cleaning.*

The women around the table were politely nodding. Great. Pity nods. So much for being a new woman. She was just the same old Riley.

"I actually enjoy a good clean," Rachel chirped. "It's a stress reliever."

"So you clean *and* bake to relieve stress? Screw Hunter, will you marry *me*?" Cat joked.

"You bake?" Riley asked as she turned to Rachel.

"I do," she replied, excitedly. She then began to tell her all about the bakery she owned in town. It was called Fairy Baked. *Great name.* And she could tell by the sheer enthusiasm pouring out of the woman as she discussed her creations, that the cakes tasted just as good as they sounded.

"I, um, I don't bake or anything, but I like to cook."

That one sentence was enough to turn the whole lunch around. For Riley anyway. Between sips of orange and bites of burger, Rachel and Riley were talking all things food. Favorite dishes, secret ingredients and fun flavor combinations. Speaking to someone so passionate about food was refreshing. It made conversation easy. And enjoyable.

Look at you go.

Yes. Look at her go. Maybe she was a new woman after all.

***

Still on a high from her lunch with the girls, Riley was ready for more social interaction. Tonight's interaction came with perks too. *Fingers crossed.*

"Where are we going?" Riley asked Wade, possibly too late as they pulled up in front of a barn.

Her question was met with dimples. "You'll see, petal. Come on." Wade climbed out of the driver's seat and rounded the truck. Opening her door, he took her hand and led her toward the ominous red building.

Walking through the thick, panelled door, she certainly wasn't expecting a restaurant. An empty one at that.

Fairy lights hung from the rafters, while colored uplights shone in each corner. Chunky wood tables and benches were scattered everywhere but it was the one in the centre that caught her eye. Adorned with flickering candles and a vase filled with wildflowers, it was like something out of a movie.

When she turned to look at Wade, he was studying her.

"I called ahead, made sure we wouldn't be in the middle of a crowded restaurant this time."

There was no crowd. No other diners. And apparently no staff. They were alone.

Heaven.

She started to wonder how she got so lucky as her hand was being tugged again. This time toward the centre table.

As they took their seat, a waiter pushed through the double doors located at the back of the barn. In mere seconds he was by their side, ready to pass them menus and ask what drinks they would like. Riley let Wade order for them as she perused the menu, where there was another surprise waiting for her.

"It's farm to table!" she squealed in delight.

"It is." Wade grinned. "I figured if we're gonna be doing this at the ranch, then we should probably taste it first."

"So you've decided…you're definitely going to do it?"

"That's the plan." His gaze dipped to the table for a second, when it returned to her, she noticed a gleam in his eyes. "You interested in helping?"

"Yes. Definitely. I'll try any food you want to feed me." She giggled. Even though she was deadly serious.

"I'll keep that in mind, darlin'. But I was actually talking about maybe helping me with things like menu creation and sourcing local produce. It's pretty damn clear you love this stuff, and you sure as hell know what you're talking about." Riley didn't bother to hide her shock. "You'd be compensated of course…for your time."

"You want to pay me?" she repeated, at the exact same time the waiter reappeared with their drinks.

Wade cleared his throat, before croaking out a "thanks." He looked strange. Almost uncomfortable.

Once the waiter disappeared, he leaned forward. His elbows meeting the table, his expression turning serious. "Pay you to consult, petal. Not for anything else. Just so we're clear."

Double freaking meanings.

Damnit, she really hated them. Why couldn't anything just mean one thing? She realized now what that weird look on his face was. Embarrassment.

She attempted to reassure him. "I know you don't want to pay me for sex."

The swig of beer Wade had just taken was promptly sprayed across the wood.

He barked out a laugh shortly after.

"That's good to know, darlin'," he drawled, moments later, still smiling. "Now we've got that cleared up, what do you think about helping me with the restaurant?"

He was being serious. He wanted her help. Her expert

opinion. Well, more like non-expert opinion.

"You don't have to pay me," she sputtered. "I'll help for free. I mean, I'm not a chef or a professional or anything. I'm just a maid."

Wade's head tilted, his astute blue stare considering her. After a good minute of looking his fill, he spoke again. "You're more than just a maid, you know that right, Riley?"

Did she know that? No. Probably not. Likely because she'd always been 'just a maid'. Firstly, at her uncle's motel and now at the Evans ranch. But that was okay. *Wasn't it?*

Undecided, she remained quiet. Prompting Wade to speak again.

"Granted, we've not known each other very long, but from the very first conversation we had about food, I could see just how much love you have for it. You light up, Riley. It's beautiful to watch."

She stayed silent, even more unsure of how to reply. It didn't matter though, Wade wasn't done.

"Is there a reason why you didn't pursue it…as a career I mean?"

Yes.

"It's, uh, it's," *complicated.* "Culinary school is expensive." That was true. "And my parents were, are," *protective to the point of suffocation*, "well, I didn't want to be too far away from them. I'm an only child and they can be…" she drifted off, not wanting to lie but also not wanting to admit at just how smothering her parents were.

Wade dipped his head, a look of understanding making his eyes squint.

"I do like learning though," she continued. "I watch the cooking channel *a lot*. And I've read a million books. I don't mind that it's not my full-time job, as long as I get to cook at home." She ended with a shrug. Like it was all fine. But now her words were out there, she was questioning how true they were.

What would her life look like if she had become a chef? It was a thought she couldn't seem to shake especially as mouthwatering aromas drifted in from the kitchen. She wasn't the only one in her head, Wade too appeared contemplative.

Snap out of it.

Yes. Inner Riley was right. Enough dwelling. More dating. Picking up the menu again, she began to read.

They had the typical seasonal salads and heirloom vegetables. Fresh chicken, beef, pork and lamb. But there was plenty of things they hadn't thought of. Like seasonal soups, a range of dairy, or something as simple as homemade bread with local butter or olive oil.

Her mind was racing as her gaze dipped to the house-made preserves. There was so much they could do. She already had a million ideas.

"I want to try the herb-crusted lamb." Her eyes met Wade's as soon as her head lifted. "I want to make the menu for you."

He broke into another wide smile. "Done. And done."

Once they'd ordered their food, talk turned to Riley's day off. In which she told Wade all about her lunch. However, a tinge of jealousy coursed through her when he mentioned he'd been set up with Cat on a date, when she'd first arrived in town. She was certain he noticed, as he was quick to confirm nothing ever happened between them. And they didn't even get a chance to order off the menu before Cody, who was now Cat's husband, barged in and carried her out of the restaurant. It all sounded very dramatic.

By the time their dinner arrived, Riley was ready to talk food again. Especially after getting a taste of the herbaceous sauce.

"We should have dishes with farm-grown grains. Artisan bread. Seasonal desserts. And we should look at getting in local wines and craft beer."

"Okay." Wade smiled. "But bear in mind we need the basics first. Cost-effective, healthy meals for the staff. Then we can start introducing fancier stuff like that for the guests."

Riley was nodding her head but secretly thinking about her recipe for fruit cobbler.

"Okay. I can do that."

"I know you can."

She believed him. More than she believed herself.

CHAPTER TWELVE

Wade was back on Riley's porch. The flickering lights from the path, not the only thing shining bright. She was glowing. Had been all night.

Despite the glow, he could see that she was nervous. She wanted him to come inside but she didn't know how to ask. It shouldn't turn him on how flustered she was becoming. But it did. His heart rate spiking so much that he could feel the veins in his neck pulse.

Leaning into her, one hand went to her hip, while the other went to the trailer door behind her. He let his mouth hover over her ear, relishing in her quiver as his warm breath hit her.

"Tell me what you're thinking." He kept his mouth over her ear. His lips grazing it every now and again. The heave of Riley's chest growing harder as she pushed against his shirt.

"That I…I want you to come inside," she whispered into the night.

"And what do you want me to do once I'm inside, petal?" She didn't reply. Not with words anyway. Her body began to melt into his, soft curves shooting fire into his veins. But it wasn't enough. He needed to hear her. "Say it."

"I," she paused. He let her take her time, his teeth scraping all the way down to her earlobe, his heart now hammering as she mewed. "I-I," she paused again. "I want you to take me. Like you did before. And…and tell me what to do."

"Good girl." Another shiver. She liked being called that. *Noted.*

Slowly, he let his mouth drag down her neck, inhaling oranges as he went. Riley threw her head back on a moan, giving him access to suck the sweet spot just above her collarbone.

It had only been a day since he'd had her in his bed, yet he felt like a starving man as he sucked and scraped. His cravings only getting stronger as she surrendered to him, her body becoming pliant beneath his touch.

Aching to feel her lips, his head lifted, and with a swoop he was tasting the berries she'd had for dessert.

Pressing into her further, he waited until she was propped up against the door before his hand drifted down to find the hem of her dress.

"Spread for me." He sacrificed her lips for one second as he spoke into her. Before capturing her again once she'd given him access.

His fingers teased the inside of her thigh, stroking up and down and up again. Wade swallowed another moan as he continued to play. When his fingers slid inside her panties, it was his turn to groan as he was met with wet heat.

Goddamn.

Knowing she was slick and ready for him only made him more impatient.

One digit slipped inside her, then two, as his thumb circled her most sensitive spot. That's when he lost her lips as her head drew back and her mouth dropped open. The evening air pierced by the sound of ragged breaths and pleading whimpers.

"That's it." His voice was rough. "Take it like a good girl." Another moan escaped into the night. "Can you take another finger, petal?"

"Yes," she whined, her eyes squeezing shut.

He let out a grunt as his third finger stretched her while she rocked against him. She was chasing her pleasure. And that was really fucking hot.

His intention was to take her to the edge. Hear her beg. But as her cries grew louder, he realized he didn't want to wait. He needed to feel her come undone.

More purrs made his blood heat as his thumb pressed harder. And when he let his fingers curl, he felt her clench around him.

"I'm gonna...I'm..."

He kissed her hard. Catching her cry as she shattered beneath him. Her body trembled, fingers clutching at his waist, while he kissed her like he owned every breath.

When he finally drew back and removed his hand, he didn't know who looked the most upset, him or her. Those big brown eyes were pleading for more and he didn't want to wait a second longer to give it to her.

"Inside, darlin'." He lifted his chin toward the door handle.

She got the message. Her keys were out, the lock was turned, and soon enough, Wade was following her into the living room. Illuminated by a single lamp, his gaze straight away went to the generously padded sofa. It looked damn inviting.

Riley turned to him; her eyelids heavy as she awaited her next instruction. He didn't say anything though. He wanted her mouth. So he took it. Her taste on his tongue moments later as he walked her backward toward the royal blue cushions.

As her calves hit the couch, their kiss turned more urgent. Driven by a need so strong, it even shocked him. It was a desperate intensity he'd never felt before. And he already ached for more.

He couldn't wait any longer. His hand went to the back of her dress where he tugged on the zip. Once opened, he carefully guided the straps over her shoulders, before letting the fabric skim her silky skin until it pooled at her feet.

Slowly breaking away from her soft lips, he spoke into her. "Turn around and place your knees on the couch."

Feeling her breath catch did nothing for his patience. Nor did the sight of her dutifully obeying him.

God-fucking-damn.

He was practically drooling as black panties struggled to contain her perfectly rounded ass. Running his hand over his head, he was torn between what to do first. He wanted it all.

Dropping to his knees, he made his decision. Gently, he dragged the thin material down her thighs, stopping when it reached her knees. It was time for dessert.

***

It was one in the morning and while he fully expected to be curled up with a naked Riley around about now, he had to admit he was enjoying watching her make fajitas just as much.

Their late-night snack was a well-deserved treat. They'd sure as hell burned off a whole lot of calories over the past few hours.

She looked damn sexy tossing meat and vegetables in the pan, and not just because she was only dressed in a thin t-shirt. But because he'd never seen her happier or more relaxed. She was sparkling.

Once Riley began preparing the tortillas, Wade went about setting the tiny table for them and poured them both some juice.

In no time at all, piping hot fajitas were being placed in front of him.

"I added some jalapeños and lime for an extra kick," Riley excitedly gushed as she pulled up a chair next to him.

As soon as the mouthwatering spices hit his nostrils, his stomach growled. "So, is this your go-to midnight snack?" he asked before taking a big bite.

Riley beamed, "One of them. Next time I'll make you

my truffle popcorn."

Wade managed to grin despite a mouthful of meat. When he was done chewing, his tone turned cheeky. "Next time, huh?"

Her neck started to flush. "Oh, um, I mean, if there is a next time. I mean, if you want to."

Is she joking?

"Petal..." He gently brushed his thumb across her lip, wiping away a smudge of sauce, his touch lingering until her eyes held him hostage. "Not only do I want there to be many, many next times, I also want to be able to call you my girl."

"Your girl?"

"Yeah, darlin'. *My girl. My woman. My girlfriend.* Whatever you wanna call it. I just want you to be mine...so...what do you say?"

The flush had spread to her cheeks now. "Yes. I say yes," she exclaimed before practically jumping out of her seat and into his arms.

Wade held her tight. Their hearts beating in harmony as he drunk in the overwhelming warmth and comfort he felt every time she was close.

After a few minutes, he mumbled into her hair. "These fajitas are really fucking good."

Riley giggled into him. "Is that why you want me to be your girlfriend...so I'll make you more fajitas?"

"Well, yeah." He grinned. "That and the sex."

She pulled back just enough to smack him in the chest. He used the opportunity to capture her lips, their laughter fading as the air charged and their slow, burning kiss stole both their breaths.

It was too soon to get excited. It had only been four dates. But Wade *was* excited. Had been since the moment he'd set eyes on her. Getting to know her, and finding out she was just as beautiful on the inside had solidified their connection. And he already knew, he didn't want to let her go.

Riley was the one to pull back, a twinkle in deep brown eyes as she said, "You're gonna have to wait until I've eaten my fajitas before we can do that again."

Wade barked out a laugh while safely depositing her from his lap to her chair. "Alright, I suppose I can wait until we've finished."

He waited for Riley to tuck back into the food before he took his next bite. Somehow, it tasted even better.

Once they'd satisfied their stomachs, there was one question Wade had been dying to know the answer to. He'd waited, hoping that Riley would open up, but he didn't want to wait any more.

"I gotta ask…how is it that a woman as gorgeous as you has never…never been with anyone?"

Riley was quiet for a while. Understandably. He let her take her time.

When she finally spoke, her voice was low. "I guess I grew up quite sheltered."

"Sure, darlin', I get that. But there's sheltered and then there's—"

"A thirty-year-old virgin?" she finished for him, her small smile fleeting.

Wade swallowed hard. "We don't have to talk about it if you don't want to."

He wasn't sure he meant that, but he was trying to be a gentleman. Although he didn't really feel like much of one. Taking her virginity in his truck was one thing, but going from that to some kind of dominant forty-eight hours later was playing on his conscience.

She asked you to tell her what to do.

She did. However, they could have gone slower. He could have held back.

"It's okay," Riley said. "I guess it's a combination of things. My parents were strict, and I lived at home right up until I moved to Woodvalley." Her gaze flicked between the wooden surface and Wade. "I worked at my uncle's motel. So when I wasn't with my parents, I was with my uncle.

Throw in a good dose of social anxiety—and your virginity is pretty much guaranteed to stick around."

"So you've never dated anyone before?" She shook her head. "Are your parents religious?" She shook her head again.

He was still looking for answers. How strict could they possibly be and why?

As if reading his mind, she went on to answer his question. "My cousin went missing when I was young—she was okay, but my parents just kind of switched after that. They wouldn't let me out of their sight."

Bingo.

"So they weren't strict before that?" She shook her head again, a flicker of sadness dulling her shine. "I take it they're not too pleased with your move out of town?"

"That's putting it mildly." Riley pushed her phone across the table and urged him to look at the screen.

Twenty missed calls. Three voicemails. And six messages.

Holy shit.

"They call me twice a day. Once in the morning, once in the evening. If I don't answer, this is what happens."

That's fucking madness.

A strange feeling came over him. The urge to fix this. Although he had no idea how. Yet the feeling penetrated deep. He wanted to make her life better. Had to. She deserved to have a life. She deserved freedom without guilt.

"Call them," he said, just as surprised at himself as she was.

"I-I don't think that's a good idea. It's one in the morning."

Maybe not. But a part of him wanted them to know that not only was she safe, but she was also with him and would be for the foreseeable future.

That's not at all possessive and slightly worrying!

"It is. And they're worried. Call them and let them know you're okay."

She picked up her phone, and hesitated. Looking between the screen and Wade several times before making the call.

"Uh, hi, Mom." Riley looked nervous as she nodded to herself. "Yeah. I'm okay. I was, uh, I was out."

Wade put out his hand and gestured for the phone. He tried not to smile as panic filled her eyes.

"Hi, Mrs Clark." He heard a gasp, before a rather annoyed sounding voice greeted him back.

"Who are you?"

"Wade Evans, ma'am. It's nice to finally talk to you, Riley's told me a lot about you."

The line went silent. Wade gazed up to find panic still clear on Riley's beautiful face as her mouth hung open.

"Has she now?" Mrs Clark replied. "And why has my daughter been talking about me to you? While you're at it, you can also explain who you are and what exactly you are doing with her in the early hours of the morning?"

"I'm her boyfriend, ma'am. Seems only right that we talk about each other's families. And in regard to why I'm with her…I'm just making sure she gets home safe and sound after our date tonight."

He waited patiently for a response. Then waited some more.

Eventually, her mother replied, rather curtly, "Please pass the phone back to my daughter."

"Sure thing, Mrs Clark. You have a good night now," he chirped before handing the phone back.

Downing his drink, he waited for Riley to finish up the call. He could tell her mother had a lot to say as she barely got a word in other than "yes" and "okay."

Once she was finished, she looked no less stressed.

"So, um, my parents want to meet you next week. They've invited us over for lunch."

Perfect.

It was what he was hoping for. Which is what he told her. She wasn't nearly as enthused as he was, though.

"Come on, petal. Time to cuddle." He pulled her to a stand, and slowly led them back over to the bed.

It was time to sleep.

CHAPTER THIRTEEN

Riley looked around at her tiny kitchen. It wasn't the most practical place to cook, but it would have to do. Ever since Wade had asked her to create a menu for him, she'd been so excited to start.

Today was the day. She had the whole day off and no plans.

After a trip to the local supermarket, Farm and Fresh, this morning, her trailer was brimming with ingredients.

As the Evans ranch raised cattle, there was plenty of access to beef and dairy, so that seemed like a good place to start.

The first recipe she wanted to test out was beef and goats cheese croquettes with a red pepper coulis to go with it.

After chopping her onions, she pulled out her mixing bowl and began combining shredded beef, goats' cheese and garlic.

She let out a blissful sigh as she mixed. It had been too long since she'd done this. The kitchen was her happy place. Her escape.

Talking of which, her phone was vibrating again. Her mom was losing her shit. Ever since Wade had spoken to her, her calls had turned hourly.

This time, she let it ring. Her mom would just have to wait. Nothing was going to spoil her day. Or her week. Life was good. For once. Amazing sex. An actual boyfriend who looks like he's just stepped out of a Wranglers commercial. And an opportunity to do what she loves and create a whole menu from scratch.

It's about time I had some good damn luck.

Riley went from creating croquettes to beef carpaccio. But when it came time to take a crack at her short rib ravioli, her trailer door rattled from a hard knock.

Who the hell is that?

For a brief and very disturbing second, she had visions of her mother tracking her down to tell her off for ignoring her calls.

No. Can't be.

Slowly walking toward the banging, she hoped she wasn't right. A minute later, she swung open the door to find out.

"Hi!" Rachel's voice squeaked. "I hope you don't mind me stop…oh my gosh, what's that amazing smell? Are you cooking?"

Riley couldn't hide her delight from the compliment and ushered Rachel inside. "I'm working on a menu for the ranch restaurant," she explained. "Do you want to try what I've made so far?"

"Uh, is the grass green?"

"What?"

"Yes, sugar." Rachel's smile softened. "I want to try what you've made."

Riley led her through to the kitchen and right into the wooden stool beside her tiny table. She then began filling a plate for her new friend.

Once she'd set down the food, she pulled up a chair opposite and anxiously awaited Rachel's reaction.

"You're staring," Rachel said politely.

"I am."

"Can we maybe, possibly, dial it back a bit, sugar? I think my boobs are sweating from the pressure."

That was graphically honest. And a reminder that she

needed to work on social boundaries. Or lack of them. To be fair to herself, she was still getting used to this whole talking to people thing.

"S-sorry," she stuttered. "I don't usually…I'm not used to…" she trailed off as Rachel gently reached out and covered her hand over Riley's.

"Hey," she said softly, "you're good. There's no need to be nervous. I don't bite, I promise…unless of course you look as delicious as one of these croquettes!" A dazzling smile took over Rachel's pretty face.

Why was she being so nice? All of the women had been. Bella, Cat and Rachel. Riley had no doubt Libby was just as kind. That didn't mean it wasn't odd though. It wasn't often she felt welcome anywhere, let alone in the company of others.

Proving Riley's point, Rachel didn't rush her to answer, or even acknowledge her words. Instead, she started eating. Satisfying noises filling her tiny trailer seconds later.

"Wow," Rachel exclaimed through a mouthful of beef and potato. "These are freaking incredible."

That felt good. She'd only ever really cooked for her parents before. So really, she had no idea if her food was palatable. Because parents lie.

Wade liked your fajitas.

He did. But they'd also spent three hours working up an appetite beforehand. So again, he could have just been happy to have sustenance.

"Thank you," she replied. "Here, try the carpaccio." She pushed another plate in front of Rachel and may have been staring again.

"You don't have to ask me twice." Rachel giggled before helping herself to a large forkful of the paper-thin slices.

More contented hums filled the kitchen. And more compliments came. The compliments didn't make her uncomfortable like they normally would though. These made her proud.

So proud, Riley decided she deserved to tuck in too and

take a break.

Her mind raced as she took bite after bite. As tasty as these dishes were, they erred on the side of fancy. Which meant they were more for guests. She realized then that her next dish needed to be something heartier, to keep the ranch hand's energy up. Short-rib ravioli would have to wait.

"What do you think of beef and cheddar beer chilli with cornbread croutons?"

"I say *yes please*!" Rachel squealed. "And where is it?"

"I think I'm going to make it now," Riley said as she pushed up off the chair. "Wanna help?"

Rachel excitedly jumped up and rolled up the sleeves to her sweater. "Where do you want me?"

Riley couldn't believe her luck. Not only did she have yet another new friend, but she had one she could cook with.

Yep. Life was good.

***

It didn't take long for Riley to remember why she hadn't been excited for today's lunch with her parents. Or why she'd purposely spent the week trying not to think about it.

Within only a minute of arriving, Wade's grilling started. Her dad was firing question after question at him, and they'd yet to even sit down at the table.

Poor Wade.

I bet he's wishing he was working right now.

It was a Saturday, so they'd both had to take the afternoon off. And after spending the whole week apart, Riley could think of so many other ways they could be spending their time.

"Dad." She sighed. Utterly mortified at her father's latest question.

Really, what she should have said was 'I think Wade's *intentions* right now are to sit down before you ask him any more ridiculous questions.' But she didn't. Because the same thing happened every time she was around her parents; she felt smaller. Her voice even quieter than normal.

A therapist would have a field day with you!

Wade turned to her then and took her hand, an easy-going smile softening his square jawline. "It's okay, petal. It's only natural for a father to be curious about his daughter's boyfriend." *Curious my ass. He's trying to scare you off.* Returning his attention to her dad, Wade continued to blow her mind. "As you know, Riley's a very special woman. I knew that very early on. And like any man who wanders upon something special…they'd be considered rather dumb if they were to let it go."

While she struggled to get her breathing under control, Wade and her father's silence was deafening. She watched on as they eyed each other. Each exchanging hard and unreadable expressions. Was this some sort of super-secret macho communication? If so, she didn't like it. And she really didn't like the feel of her belly flipping as the silence dragged on.

"Let's take a seat, shall we?" her mother chimed, breaking the stalemate and directing the men toward their modest pine dining table. "We don't want the food to get cold."

No, we wouldn't want that, Riley thought as she rolled her eyes. A part of her was worried she'd miss her parents once she'd moved, after all, she'd never known anything else, but how wrong she was. Being back at her childhood home was already making every breath heavier.

Maybe I'm allergic to my mother's hideous paisley wallpaper?

Whatever it was, air was still struggling to flow from her lungs to her throat as she took her seat at the table. Next to Wade. His hand sliding straight to her thigh, where his palm lightly brushed over her in a soothing motion. Just that small gesture managed to ease some of the tension that had been enough to snap her spine straight.

The awkward silence lingered well into their lunch. It was only after Riley had finished her mashed potatoes that her dad spoke again.

"So, Wade, have you ever been married?"

What kind of question was that?

"No, sir." Wade didn't look the slightest bit bothered as he continued to pile chicken fried steak onto his fork.

"Any kids?"

Seriously?

"No, sir." Again, Wade shrugged off the question.

Her dad hummed to himself before adding, "And why is that do you think? I mean, you must be, what, mid-thirties, right? Most men your age are married by now, starting families."

Oh my God. I can't believe this is happening.

She didn't know what had come over her father. She'd never seen him act so rudely. Or spoken to anyone the way he was speaking to Wade. Not that she'd ever brought a man home before for him to interrogate. Or anyone for that matter.

"I guess I just hadn't met the right woman yet, sir." Wade twisted to look at Riley, dimples making it impossible for her not to return his sweet smile. "I certainly hadn't paid Silver Valley a visit."

Riley's chest squeezed. A week without seeing him had given her plenty of time to overthink their relationship. And second guess if he really had been too busy with work to make time to see her. Really, she had no reason to doubt him, especially as she stared into aqua eyes and saw nothing but sincerity staring back at her.

"So, you think my daughter's the one for you, is that it?" her dad haughtily replied.

That was enough. No more. She found her voice.

"Stop," the command was as forceful as she could manage. "Leave him alone." *Deep breaths, you can do this.* "I didn't bring Wade here to be spoken to like this."

"Why did you bring him here?" Her mother was the one to respond to her shaky outburst.

Oh, I don't know, maybe because normal parents want to get to know their daughter's boyfriend. Are happy that their child is happy.

114

And maybe, just maybe, don't treat new people with visible disdain.

Of course she didn't say that. She didn't say anything. As quickly as her confidence had come, it disappeared just as fast at the sight of her mom's narrowed gaze.

Wade didn't leave her hanging though. His hand on her thigh squeezed. "I wanted to meet you," he announced. "I know it's not been long since Riley and I met, but I care a great deal about her." Her attention went to his perfectly chiselled jaw as he spoke. Goddamn he was fine. And he wanted *her*. Was going head-to-head with her parents for *her* after only four dates. How? Why? "I only expect my feelings for her to grow." *Sweet mother of maple syrup.* "Which means it's only right I meet her parents."

She had no doubt her parents were frowning. Eying Wade with open hostility. But she didn't care. Everything they'd thrown at him. All the damn questions. The lack of basic manners. Wade hadn't even flinched. Not only that, but every answer he'd calmly given only made her fall for him harder. It was that reason that she did what she did next.

Bringing her hand up, she let her knuckles drag over his stubble until he turned to face her. Slowly lifting her butt from the velour seat, she lay a soft kiss on his lips. It was short and sweet. Before pulling back, she whispered, "Thank you."

His gaze remained locked on her as the room around them blurred. And when his chin dipped and callused fingers skimmed her cheek, she knew she no longer cared about her parent's approval. When their lips met again, the kiss he gave her was claiming. Firm and fierce. And more than enough to make her pulse pound.

Her eyes were still glazed as Wade drew back. Faintly she heard her father grumble, but it wasn't enough to garner her attention. Not when the man next to her was looking at her with fire in his eyes.

It was time to go. No matter how much time they stayed, her parents had already proved they didn't care to get to know Wade. Or welcome him into their home.

Managing to find her voice for the second time today, she rose from her seat. Standing tall as she flicked her head in the direction of her mother and father who were now gawking at her.

"Mom, Dad, thank you for lunch. We're going to get going now. It's a long drive back to Woodvalley and we have dinner plans that we really can't miss."

It wasn't that long a drive. They would be back in two hours tops. But that wasn't the point. The point was, she was done. She'd moved out. And she didn't have to deal with any of this anymore.

Wade stood next, taking her hand in his as he too turned toward her parents. "Mr Clark." He nodded. "Mrs Clark." Another nod. "It was a pleasure to meet you. Thank you for such a lovely lunch."

Before they had a chance to reply, Wade was whisking Riley away, through the door and down the hallway. It seemed she wasn't the only one in a hurry to leave.

CHAPTER FOURTEEN

Wade's blood pressure was still dangerously high as he held open his front door and gestured for Riley to enter. He was expecting her parents to be difficult, but he hadn't expected his woman to shrink into herself in their presence. That pissed him off. Being with family is supposed to be safe. She should be free to be herself. And be accepted.

Instead, he'd witnessed judgement, blatant hostility and two people desperate for control over their adult daughter's decisions. Thank God she'd moved to Woodvalley when she did, he couldn't imagine her living her life to its fullest while in that house.

He watched as Riley furiously rubbed her wrist, which was enough to get him moving. In two big strides, he was in front of her, untangling her hand and bringing it to his lips.

"Petal," he rumbled. "It's going to be okay. I promise."

Despite a confident exit from her parent's house, Riley had grown quiet on their drive back home. She'd also apologised to him several times. Clearly, she was horrified by her parent's behaviour.

"How can you say that?" She slumped, looking just as dejected as she sounded. "I should have stayed and spoken to them. Left on better terms. I feel so bad."

Which is probably exactly what they wanted. More guilt

to try and control her with. He kept that thought to himself as he gently cupped her cheek.

"Why did you move here, darlin'?"

Riley blinked, momentarily thrown by the change of subject.

"Uh, I-I wanted a change, I guess. Something just for me."

"That's what I thought. It's time to put yourself first. And that's exactly what you did today."

"And you," she whispered.

His thumb which had been lazily stroking her silky skin, stilled. "What do you mean?"

Big brown eyes stared up at him. "I didn't like them speaking to you like that. You don't deserve that. You were nothing but polite to them." Her voice was still quiet, as if she were sharing a secret.

"I don't want that beautiful head of yours to worry about me, petal. You're the important one. Remember that." His thumb started moving again, this time swiping her plump bottom lip.

He watched as her eyes glazed. The familiar look of want already heating his blood. Need churning in his gut. It had been a whole goddamn week since he'd tasted her soft, supple skin.

Stupid, damn barn conversion.

"Fair warning." His tone was about as rough as his heartbeat. "One more look like that, baby, and in five seconds, I'm gonna have you pinned to the nearest surface, screaming my name."

The flash of desire in her eyes told him everything he needed to know. That and the swipe of her tongue across his thumb.

Fuck me.

This woman had already crawled so deep under his skin, he couldn't ever imagine being able to resist her. Which was scary as hell.

Wade inched closer, his free hand wrapping around her

waist while his other hand disappeared into long black hair. With one tug, her body was plastered to his and the taste of oranges hit his tongue even before his mouth came crashing down onto hers.

Urging her back, he took the kiss deeper, his fingers already itching to make the moans he was swallowing louder. Wilder.

By the time they hit the wall, he couldn't wait any longer. Breaking away, he spun her around, his mouth going to her ear as he tugged her hips against him.

"Hands against the wall." Even he noticed the raw, heated need in his voice. "Good girl."

She shivered at his words, and continued to shake as he traced the shell of her ear with his tongue.

"I've missed you." His mouth slowly glided down her neck. "Want me to show you how much?" His hips bucked as a sexy mewl left her lips.

Enough fucking around.

His hand went to the zipper on the back of her dress. He was ready to make good on his promise.

***

Just like every night last week, Wade was back at the barn tonight. Ever since they'd found out the mild fall weather was set to turn stormy earlier than usual this year, it had been all hands on deck. While he and his brothers may not be builders, there was plenty to do on site to help quicken up the work being done.

Tonight, his brother Zach had roped in a few of his friends from the fire station to chip in too.

"I met your woman the other week." Benny grinned as he held the roll of insulation up against the wall.

"Come again?" Wade paused mid-staple.

"I met Riley," Benny repeated, giving him a look that suggested Wade was a dumb fuck. "Your woman. She's hot."

Attempting to tamper down his jealousy, his focus went back to the staple gun in his hand as he continued on with their task. Putting a bit more force behind each staple.

"I'd appreciate it if you didn't comment on my woman's appearance. Unless you're looking to get my fist in your face."

Benny threw his head back and laughed. Loudly. And when he caught Wade's scowl, his laugh only got more obnoxious.

"What's so funny?" Luke sauntered up to them both. Passing Benny more rolls of insulation he'd cut to size.

"Honestly, I don't know what's funnier," Benny said through the last of his chuckles. "The way you guys start threatening violence every time you fall for a woman. Or how quickly you all get pussy whipped."

Wade was unimpressed with the man's reply. Seeing as it was also a dig at Luke, he didn't look all that pleased with his friend either. Hence the death stare.

Luke's expression went from deathly glare to mischievous grin a minute later as he turned to Wade. "You know anything about Benny's high school sweetheart? Think her name was Bethany something."

"Luke," Benny warned. His demeanour no longer jovial, his jaw tightly clenched.

Was it wrong that Wade was enjoying this? Probably. And he only enjoyed it more as he too smiled and confirmed he knew exactly who Luke was talking about. "Bethany Mayer."

"You two better shut the fuck up now," Benny cautioned. Sounding more like a sulky schoolboy than anything remotely menacing.

Luke let out a low whistle. "Don't tell me you're about to threaten violence, Benny boy?" he teased, unable to fully contain a snigger.

Matt was next to join the group. "What's going on?"

Wade threw his hands up and excused himself, not about to bring his brother in on the man's misery. As much as he loved watching Benny eat his words, he knew a broken heart when he saw one.

"Benny here is—" Luke started but Wade interrupted, taking pity on the poor man.

"He thinks Riley's hot." Wade didn't miss the gratitude in Benny's eyes when they swung to him.

"And you're still breathing?" Matt chuckled after smacking Benny on the back. He knew his older brother all too well it would seem.

"Yeah, well, we need this insulation fitted, don't we? Otherwise, all bets would be off." Wade grunted before picking up the next roll of lining.

Luke scoffed but chose not to call them out. Instead, he decided Wade was a better target. "I hear you met the parents this weekend." He grinned. "You'll be moving her into your house next."

"Says the man who moved Bella into his home after a week," Wade returned; a smug smile plastered all over his face.

A resounding "oooh" from Benny and Matt only made his grin stretch further, while Luke narrowed his eyes. "Bella moved in after two months, dude, and you know it."

"Officially, sure." Wade shrugged. "But I also happen to know you asked her to move her stuff from our guest cabin to your house a week in."

Bella was going to kill him. But it was worth it as he watched steam come out of Luke's ears. All the while Benny was making whipping noises and Matt was doubled over laughing.

"What's with all you guys," Matt spluttered. "You're all way too desperate to be tied down if you ask me!"

Wade wondered if his brother realized what a crazy thing that was to say. Especially as he'd been with his girlfriend longer than any man in the room had been with their women.

"Speaking of which." Zach joined them. "When are you gonna make an honest woman out of Melody?"

Matt not so subtly rolled his eyes. "Not all of us are destined for marriage."

"Oh yeah, Melody know that?" Wade chipped in.

What the hell was his brother playing at? Melody was a good woman. He shouldn't be leading her on.

"She's not expecting a ring anytime soon if that's what you're asking," Matt replied.

It was met with crossed arms from Zach, a "dude" from Benny, and a headshake from Luke.

"You've been together five years." Luke pinned Matt with a look that clearly stated, 'you're a dumbass.'

The man wasn't wrong.

"And?"

"*And?*" Luke mocked, "if you don't see a future with the girl, what the hell are you doing together?"

It was a good fucking question. One that Wade was thankful he didn't have to ask.

"You a relationship expert now, man? After all of, what, four months?"

Zach and Wade's lips twitched, but Benny was the only one laughing as he backhanded Luke's stomach and cried, "Ooo, burn!"

It was true that Luke probably wasn't the best person to be dishing out relationship advice, seeing as he had never actually had one until Bella came along.

And you're much better?

He wasn't. Which is why he was glad someone else had called Matt out on his bullshit.

Not one to back down, Luke's eyes twinkled as he calmly took a step forward. "I'm not claiming to be an expert by any means. Having said that though, before Bella, I never made any promises to anyone. I was honest with any woman who came my way. Then, when I met the right woman, that's when I made a commitment."

Benny was animated again, this time low whistling between sniggers.

"What's with the mother's meeting? We've got shit to

do." Jonah was next to join the group, followed shortly by Hunter, another one of Zach's friends.

Benny filled the newcomers in. In more detail than necessary. And much to Matt's dismay if the palm in his face was anything to go by.

"You done?" Matt snarked. "Like my brother said, we've got shit to do. So, unless you want to dish out any more unwarranted advice, I'll be getting back to work."

No one uttered a word as Matt stormed off, but there were plenty of looks exchanged. It wasn't like his brother to get angry. He was normally the one winding everyone up, not being wound himself.

Shit. Somethings going on.

Wade clearly needed to talk to him. Now wasn't the time though. Not when he had access to power tools. His brotherly advice would have to wait.

***

Wade's gut churned as he reread the message Riley had just sent him.

Riley: Can we talk?

He still didn't know how three simple words could feel like such a punch to the stomach, yet they did.

Trying his best to think back over the past few days, he wondered if he'd missed something. They'd spent the whole weekend together after their visit to her parents. She'd been in his bed two nights in a row. Then on Monday she'd had plans with Bella, so they didn't see each other. And now it was Tuesday. He was coming up blank. Nothing drastically changed since he kissed her goodbye yesterday morning.

"Everything okay?" Matt asked as he eyed the phone that was still in Wade's hand.

"Yeah." He waved him off before slipping the device back into his pocket.

Not forgetting what had happened at the barn last night,

Wade had invited Matt to lunch. They were currently sat in Molly's red booths, digging into delicious food.

"So." Wade's elbows hit the metal table as he leaned forward. But he didn't get any more words out as Matt was quick to cut him off.

"So?" Matt eyed him suspiciously. "So...what?"

He wasn't going to make this easy it would seem.

"What was that the other night?"

"What was what the other night?" Was Matt's smartass reply.

Wade sighed, not hiding his frustration. "You gonna answer every question I ask with a question?"

"Maybe," his brother scoffed. "That all depends on what fucking inane questions you plan on asking me."

Perfect. He'd be having a side of stubborn asshole with his burger.

"How about we start with what the hell is going on with you and Melody?"

"What's that supposed to mean?"

Another sigh, this one louder. "It *means*—I'm getting the distinct feeling things aren't exactly *fine and dandy*."

Matt didn't reply. Instead, his gaze traveled around the bright red and whitewashed walls of the diner. Then on to the people scattered in pleather booths along the window opposite them. After a painfully slow perusal, his eyes finally swung back to him. And when they did, Wade could see the pain.

"Talk to me," Wade said again. "What's going on?"

"I just," Matt paused, his gaze dropping to his soda glass, "I can't give her what she wants."

"And what's that?" This would be so much easier if his brother just spat it out. Both their food was getting cold.

"Same thing most chicks want," he tsked, "a ring, a house, kids and shit."

"*Kids and shit?*" Wade repeated, resisting the urge to shake his head. "So, you don't want that with her or you don't want that with anyone?"

This was like getting blood from a fucking stone.

Matt shrugged. "All I know is that I don't want it with her."

Ouch.

"Then you need to tell her."

"Oh yeah, that's gonna go *really* well. *So, Melody, I know we've been together five years and everything, but I think we should call it quits. Mostly 'cause I don't wanna marry you and I don't want you to be the mother of my children.*"

Wade flinched. That was harsh. The truth, but so dang harsh.

"There are better ways of putting it, Matt, and you know it. What else is holding you back?"

His brother was a straight shooter. It wasn't often he'd bite his tongue. Which meant there was something else stopping him from telling Melody the truth.

Matt's eyes hit the table again, this time they were on his plate as he pushed what was left of his fries to one side. "She was with me before the accident," he muttered. His voice so quiet, it could have been a whisper.

"So?"

"*So?*" Matt returned, clearly agitated. "She stuck by me. Was loyal. Don't forget, we got together when I was *someone*. A bull rider. Then after the accident, she ended up with some fucking broken cowboy. And she still stayed."

Just the mention of the accident had Wade's fists clenching. Years ago, Matt had broken his ribs in a competition, which wasn't unusual for a bull rider. That wasn't the issue. A week after he was injured, his manager convinced him to ride another rodeo because he had a sponsor coming. It was safe to say it didn't end well. In fact, his brother was lucky to be alive.

Wade downed his drink in an attempt to wash away some of the bitterness now tinging his tongue.

"You get it now?" Matt asked.

Oh, he got it alright. Good old guilt was keeping them together.

Wade clinked his glass down. "I get it. But that doesn't mean it's okay." He pinned his brother with a serious stare. "Melody doesn't give two shits about you being a bull rider. You were only together for a few months before the accident so really, for the majority of your relationship this is who you've been."

When Matt's gaze went back to his plate, Wade decided to try and lighten the mood. "I wouldn't go as far to say you're *broken* though...that's a little fucking dramatic...a rancher who's *only kind of bad* at his job maybe, but not broken."

He didn't miss his brother's lips kick up at the sides. "You're an asshole."

"Yup. You gonna talk to Melody?"

Matt nodded but didn't say anymore. That was good enough for Wade. One problem dealt with, now he had to work out what was going on with his own relationship. Talking of which, he pulled his phone out of his pocket and shot Riley a message.

Wade: On my way back to the ranch now. You still going to be doing laundry at my place this afternoon?

Three little dots appeared right away.

Riley: Yes, I'm on my way.

Wade's stomach flip-flopped. *Please don't be anything bad.* Because a one-week relationship wouldn't just be pathetic, it would be so damn typical of his luck.

CHAPTER FIFTEEN

Riley actually physically jumped as the laundry room door swung open. And after getting one look at the heat burning in Wade's eyes, her heart went from a manageable gallop to a fatal thump.

He stalked toward her like a man on a mission, and she could swear he was still moving as his arm swooped around her waist before she was hauled into him.

Within seconds, his lips slammed against hers and she was airborne. Her legs wrapping around Wade's hips as he deposited her onto the washing machine. Which just so happened to be turned on.

Holy moly.

Between the vibrations and the perfect precision of every tongue swipe, brain cells were being fried and there was a good possibility she'd never see them again. But who cared about that, there were more important things to think about, like would this be considered funny business?

As the washing machine switched to spin, she was grateful that at least a few of her moans were being drowned out. Especially as they turned more desperate. Her hands slid between them and went to his shirt where she began fumbling with buttons.

They should normalize Velcro shirt fastenings.

Finally open, a growl ripped through Wade as her fingers

glided over muscled ridges. To her disappointment, she lost his mouth just moments later. He drew back just enough to pin her with a smouldering stare.

"What is it you wanted to talk about, petal?" he asked through ragged breaths.

"What?"

"Your text," he reminded her. "You said you wanted to talk?" He was searching her eyes now, looking for something.

Right. Her text. That memory must have been burnt off with the other brain cells.

"Oh, yeah, um…" Her breaths were just as shallow as his. "I don't want to go a week without seeing you again. I know you're busy with the barn…but maybe I could help or you could come to my place when you're done or we can—" She stopped talking as his expression went from cautious to a blinding smile.

"That's it? That's what you wanted to talk about?"

"Yeah."

A short sharp laugh escaped before he continued. "Do me a favor, darlin', next time you wanna talk about something like that…maybe say a bit more in your message?"

She didn't understand. What was wrong with her message? "But I wanted to talk to you in person," she defended.

His features softened as he took her in. Then, a quick dip and he was laying a sweet, tender kiss on her lips. That was over way too fast.

"I thought you wanted to break up," he admitted. Leaving her even more confused. "*We need to talk* is usually code for *I want to break up*—in the dating world, baby."

Oh. Shit. Well, that's dumb.

Which is what she told him next. "That's a stupid code. Surely the list of things a couple talk about is never ending…what are you supposed to say when you want to talk to each other?"

Wade chuckled, laying another kiss on her, this time on her forehead. "I agree. Maybe we can come up with our own code. Something just for us."

She liked that. A lot.

"Can we get back to the funny business now?"

She could watch Wade laugh all damn day. It wasn't just the rich, velvety sound that gave her goosebumps, it was the sight of his square jaw that only became more prominent as his head was thrown back. The stubble that framed that smile. And the deepened shadows making his already perfectly masculine face just that little bit more rugged.

She was still staring when his laughter eventually subsided. So she didn't miss the switch. Or the darkening of his gaze.

"Goddamn it, Riley. You keep looking at me like that and they'll be nothing funny about what I'm gonna do to you."

A shiver of excitement ran down her spine at the ferociousness of his declaration. "What are you going to do to me?" She smiled.

Another rumble from his chest filled the small space, as his hands went to her jeans. In record time, they were undone and being pushed down her legs. Her shoes joined her trousers on the floor as Wade was back up in an instant, freeing himself from his own wranglers. Her gaze darted down, and she swallowed hard.

When she looked back up, Wade didn't hide the pure lust crackling between them.

"I'm gonna take you hard, Riley." The rough edge to his voice made the hairs on the back of her neck prick up. "You need me to stop or slow down, you tell me." She nodded as he hooked his fingers in her panties and dragged them to the side as he positioned himself at her entrance.

Her skin suddenly felt hot and tingly as her chest rose and fell faster with each breath. If she'd have known this was what sex was like, she wouldn't have waited so long to have it. Although a part of her knew that it wouldn't be the same with anyone else.

***

"Let's conversate!" Riley squeaked as her head came off Wade's chest. "That's it!"

Wade was grinning as he brushed the hair off her face. "What are you talking about, petal?"

"Our code." She matched his smile. "That's what it should be…when we want to talk but not scare the crap out of each other. *Let's conversate.* It rhymes and everything." She was feeling really pleased with herself, even more so when laughter filled the laundry room.

They were cuddled up on the porcelain tiles. Which weren't exactly comfortable but were essential as Riley wasn't sure if her legs would work if she attempted to stand. Wade wasn't kidding when he told her he was going to take her hard. Not that she was complaining.

"It's perfect," he agreed once his laughter subsided. "What you were saying before…about spending more time together this week." He paused just as her eyes widened in anticipation. "I want that. I missed you last week, more than I should admit. How do you feel about spending the weekends together, after work of course, and then a few nights a week too?"

She felt excited. Over the freaking moon. He wanted to spend every weekend with her, plus weeknights. But as quickly as happiness came, so did the nerves. Doubt crept in. What if he got bored of her? What if she ran out of things to say to him? All those nights together too, she couldn't keep waking at the crack of dawn and brushing her teeth and fixing her hair. *When will I sleep?*

"Hey." Her attention went to him again. "If it's too much…" he trailed off.

"No," she was quick to say. "It's not that."

"Then what is it?" Wade lifted his head just enough to lay a soft kiss on her cheek. "You can tell me. I won't be offended, I promise," he reassured.

She was new to all of this. She had no idea what she should or shouldn't share with someone who was her boyfriend. A part of her wanted to tell him to wait a minute while she called Bella to ask, but the other part, that part wanted to tell him everything. Surely that was the right thing. The man had just been inside of her, so really, if she was comfortable to be doing that with him, she should be comfortable enough to tell him how she's feeling.

Before she could change her mind, she bit the bullet. "I want to spend weekends together and as many weeknights as possible. But I'm scared." Wade's hand lifted; his fingers went into her hair as his thumb gently stroked her cheek. "My evenings mostly consist of reading or watching the TV, I don't know how fun I'll be. I'm not used to spending that much time with anyone. What if I'm boring...what if you get sick of me?"

"Petal," he uttered, "you have no idea how perfect you are."

What?

Riley's head shook. "I'm not," she vehemently denied. "I wake up before you and I brush my teeth, I do my hair and sometimes I even put make-up on. I don't usually look like that in the mornings. You're going to see that. What if you don't want to have sex with me again after seeing me like that?"

Wade pulled her face down. Resting her forehead against his, his tone turned serious. "Darlin', you're the most goddamn beautiful woman I've ever seen. Inside and out. And if you think for one second clean teeth and some mascara would somehow magically change the way I feel about you then I'm doing something seriously wrong."

"You're not doing anything wrong," she muttered against his lips.

"I am. I want you feeling secure. I want you knowing how fucking sexy you are. How nothing about you is boring. And not only is it not possible to get sick of you, but I also can't even imagine a moment to pass without me wanting you."

Wow. What do I even say to that?

Nothing came to her, so she stayed quiet. Breathing in musky leather cologne as her heart raced.

"I don't want to scare you, Riley, but I meant what I said to your parents…I have no intention of letting you go. You have to know that I'm all in."

She was scared alright. Scared of her feelings. How strong they already were. Scared of fucking this up. Having no clue what she was doing. But mostly, she was scared of getting hurt. She was acutely aware of how much damage this blue-eyed cowboy could do to her heart.

She nodded into him. "Don't hurt me," she whispered.

"Never," he growled before capturing her lips.

God, she hoped he was telling the truth.

***

One month into being Wade Evans's girlfriend and Riley was more confident than ever. One month ago, standing in Zach and Libby Evans's backyard for a group barbecue would have brought her out in hives, but here she stood, huddled with women she had fallen in love with.

"I can't believe you're going to be Mrs Hulk in less than six weeks!" Cat teased as she clinked hips with Rachel.

"Can you stop calling him the hulk!" Rachel playfully smacked her friend. "He's not green and his clothes don't tear off when he's angry. Well…" she giggled, "not all the time anyway."

"Talking of the wedding," Libby interjected, before Cat could make the dirty joke she was dying to make. "Have you asked Riley yet?"

Asked me what?

Rachel beamed as she turned to Riley. "No. I was waiting until after her menu tasting, but seeing as that's tomorrow, there's no time like the present." *Seriously, asked me what?* "I'd really like it, no, scrap that, I would *love* it, if you would do me the honor of being one of my bridesmaids."

Riley's jaw dropped open. Had she just heard the woman right?

"What?" she uttered. Her brain unsure she heard correctly.

"I know we haven't known each other that long," Rachel continued, "but with all the time we've been spending together, I feel like we've just gotten so close, and now I can't imagine you not being a part of my wedding. Say you'll do it?"

They had been spending a lot of time together. It was true. Rachel had been helping her with the creation of the ranch menu. And between cooking and eating not just the food she'd made but also the woman's delicious desserts, they'd got to know each other. Riley had told her all about her very sheltered childhood, her anxiety in social situations and her severe lack of friendships. And in turn, Rachel had told her all about her tumultuous past which included an abusive father, his gambling debts and how the combination of the two ended up getting her now fiancé shot.

"Yes," she breathed as tears pricked her eyes. "I would love to. If you're sure?"

Libby, Cat, Bella and Rachel all jumped in excitement. With cheers ringing around the small garden. It was enough to catch the attention of the men, who were now wandering over.

"What's going on?" Wade was the first to get there, his arm wrapping around Riley's shoulders as she was pulled into his side.

"Riley has just agreed to be a bridesmaid at my wedding," Rachel chirped.

"Yeah?" The smile Wade gave Riley was so bright, she resisted the urge to squint as he peered down at her.

"Don't you mean *our* wedding, honeybun?" Hunter teased as Rachel was hauled backward into her man's big burly arms.

Cat's husband Cody joined the group next, then Zach, both of them claiming their women with a kiss and arm wrap. Luke and Benny were next to roll up. Luke lacing his fingers through Bella's and offering her a sweet smile. Meanwhile, Benny was stuffing another hot dog into his mouth.

Matt and Jonah were the only ones who hadn't joined them as they remained around the barbecue, flipping burgers with the help of Cat and Cody's son, Dylan.

Rachel repeated the news to the newcomers. All of whom looked pleased. But it was Wade's happiness that radiated as he lay more kisses on the top of her head. He'd been extremely encouraging and supportive of her new friendships. And whenever Rachel had come over to his place, because that was where Riley spent most of her time now, he'd give them space to have their girl time.

"You wanna be a groomsman?" Hunter grunted, his chin lifting to Wade.

"Huh?" Was Wade's baffled reaction.

All the women stifled their sniggers. "Gonna need someone to walk Riley down the aisle, wanna be a groomsman?" Hunter repeated.

"Men really are a different species," Libby said as she shook her head.

Rachel was first to lose the battle and let out a giggle. Next was Bella. Then Cat. And finally, Libby and Riley joined in.

"I'll walk her down the aisle." Benny put his hand up. "In case you fuckers have forgotten, I'm not walking down the aisle with anyone."

More laughter from the group erupted.

Luke slapped Benny on the back. "We've not forgotten, dude."

"Why are you all laughing?" Benny whined.

"You've not told him yet, have you?" Rachel slapped Hunter's hand that was resting on her stomach.

"Told me what?"

Hunter turned to Benny and blanked his features as he announced, "You're walking down the aisle with Snowcone."

"The fucking cat!" Benny spat as the group exploded again. "Are you fucking kidding?"

Riley took a moment to look around at the men and women surrounding her. She never knew a life like this was possible for her. She felt accepted. For the first time in thirty years. The women knew all about her anxiety and never pushed for more than she could give. They embraced her quirks. Celebrated them. And as for the man holding her tight, without a doubt, she knew she'd fallen in love with him. But instead of letting her fear of what that meant win, she was going to lean into it. Enjoy it. She'd wasted enough time.

CHAPTER SIXTEEN

Wade stopped himself from pulling Riley into his arms. He doubted she'd appreciate the gesture after she'd gone to so much trouble trying to remain professional.

He and his brothers sat around the fold out table they'd set up in the barn. The exterior upgrades were now complete, but they still had to sort the interior. The first thing he wanted to do was get a kitchen installed for Riley.

"Okay." Her shaky smile made his chest tighten. "So, these are the main dishes I've come up with." Her hand waved over the contents of the table. Piping hot plates filled to the brim, with an aroma that was already making his stomach growl. "On the left are the staples. These will be what the staff are going to want to eat. Then here on the right are more guest focused dishes. Classics with a twist."

"This looks amazing, Riley," Zach exclaimed.

She thanked him shyly.

"Do we get to eat now?" Jonah asked before he got a thump in the chest from Wade. "Ow!"

"She's not finished yet, man," Matt informed Jonah on his behalf.

Riley jumped in, before his brother starved to death. "You can go ahead and eat. Next to each dish you'll find an ingredients list. I've also made a note of local suppliers and some rough pricing."

Damn she was good.

His brothers looked just as impressed as he was. Jonah in particular who was in charge of the books.

None of them wasted any time digging into the food. Satisfied noises echoing around the empty barn.

Matt didn't bother to swallow before asking, "What's this sauce?"

"It's a red pepper coulis," Riley replied. "I wanted something smoky but sweet that would complement the tangy goats cheese. Do you like it?"

"Do I like it?" Matt guffawed. "Sweetheart, I'm two bites away from getting down on one knee and asking you to marry me."

"Hey!" Wade shot his brother a dirty look. "You just try it…see what happens."

"Jesus." Matt laughed. "Your face! Calm down loverboy. Don't get your panties in a twist."

His panties were in a twist. Irrational jealousy had never been his thing, not until he met Riley. Now, he could easily beat his chest in anger if an unsuspecting male goes anywhere near her.

That's normal.

He was well aware it wasn't. But all he could do was at least try to not act like a caveman when the urge to beat his chest arose.

Ignoring his brother, he simply grunted and went back to his short-rib ravioli. Fucking heaven.

Contented hums continued for the next half an hour. There were only a few questions for Riley as she watched on patiently. Apprehension keeping her brows pulled together for far too long.

Wade looked to each of his brothers once they were done, his silent question acknowledged by a nod from all three men.

Jonah was the one to speak up first. "We love it, Riley. All of it. I'll need to talk to the suppliers and run the numbers…but if they work, then we'd like to move forward with this menu."

"Really?" Her elated squeal made his heart squeeze.

"Really, petal." He couldn't keep quiet any longer. "We also have a chef position open, if you're interested?"

Rounded eyes went to him, before traveling to each of his brothers. "Me? But I…" He already knew what she was going to say, and Wade and his brothers had already discussed it. The job was hers if she wanted it. "I didn't go to culinary school or anything. I've got no qualifications."

"Darlin', this feast here is all the qualifications we need." Zach's tone was gentle. "You won't be the only chef, we'll get a sous chef in too, someone who'll be able to cover days you're not working. And of course, there will be some kitchen staff to help out. But it'll be your kitchen. Your menu. You'll run it."

As soon as Wade noticed her eyes swell, he was up off his seat. Two strides later and he was pulling her into his arms as she spoke into his chest.

"I just can't believe you would take a chance on me like that." She pulled back then, peering up at him, not hiding her disbelief. "It's not because you're having sex with me, is it?"

He smiled while his brothers sniggered like schoolboys. "No, baby, I'm not offering you the job because we're having sex. Besides, it's a family business, this is a joint decision. And the last time I checked; you weren't sleeping with my brothers."

Matt cleared his throat and started to say something, but Wade beat him to it. Twisting to face him he warned, "Don't you fucking dare."

More sniggers from his brothers rang out as he turned back.

Fucking children.

"You're talented, Riley. This is what you should be doing. Seeing you in the kitchen…you shine. So fucking bright."

Riley was on her toes, her hands wrapping around Wade's neck as she tugged his head down. He was treated with a kiss so raw with emotion it stole his breath.

"Guys!" Matt sighed. "Can we at least pretend to be professional here?" Jonah and Zach were back to laughing. "We really need her to sign some sort of contract."

Wade ignored his brothers and carried on kissing his woman. There was plenty of time to be professional. Right now, though, they were celebrating.

***

"Yes, Mom, a chef."

That was the third time Wade had heard Riley say that to her mother. He was trying really hard not to get pissed off. The phone conversation he'd heard may have been one sided, but it didn't take a genius to work out her parents weren't reacting with the joy and pride Riley deserved.

Luckily, by the time Riley hung up, all it took was one look at how happy she was for his temper to wane.

Crawling onto his couch, she shuffled into him, even going as far as to lift his arm so she could shimmy under it.

"I still can't believe I'm going to be getting paid to cook." Her head dipped until she was snuggled into his chest. "Thank you," she whispered, warming his insides.

Dropping a kiss to her head, he told her for the fourteenth time today, "You don't need to thank me, petal. You got that job all on your own. At one point I thought Matt was going to cry tears of joy when he got a taste of your whipped blue cheese."

Adorable giggles vibrated against his chest.

"Now that you're officially our new chef, how do you feel about coming kitchen shopping with me and Zach next week?"

Riley jolted up, big eyes meeting his. "Really? I get to help choose?"

"It's gonna be *your kitchen*."

He must have said something right because the next thing he knew she was climbing onto his lap. Giving him a kiss so sweet, he could swear he was getting high on sugar. When she drew back, his throat clogged. It was too soon to feel what he was feeling. It had only been a month. But he felt it nonetheless.

Maybe just don't say it yet?

The last thing he wanted to do was scare her off. And with all the change coming her way over the next few months, it would be unfair for her to be distracted. He wanted her to enjoy every moment.

Besides, they were in a good place. There was no rush. He already got to see her most nights as he'd practically moved her into his house. And he wanted to enjoy every day too.

With that in mind, his fingers went around the back of her neck as he tugged her back into him. Then he went about kissing the hell out of her. Greedily lapping up every whimper as his other hand went under the thin material of her dress and straight to her ass.

It only took a few minutes of cupping supple flesh before his patience ran out. Easing back, his voice was deep as he ordered, "Clothes off."

Here's to living in the now.

CHAPTER SEVENTEEN

Riley stared at her reflection in the mirror. The long pink silk bridesmaids dress was probably the sexiest she'd ever seen. With thin straps, it managed to hug every curve and came complete with a rather revealing slit down the front that was bordering on inappropriate.

A low whistle brought her head up. Wade was standing behind her, looking awfully fine in a black suit.

"Goddamn, you look fucking hot."

Riley's gaze sliced to his in the mirror. He was giving her that look again. The one that meant he was about to either order her to drop to her knees or take her clothes off. She loved that look.

Spinning around, she took her time perusing him. Trying to work out how late they'd be if she surrendered to the heat in Wade's eyes.

"We don't have time." She smiled.

As much as she wanted him, she wasn't about to let her friend down. She may be new to having friends, but even she knew being late to a wedding is rude. And being late when you're in the wedding party is unforgivable.

"I can be quick." He winked.

That was a lie. "You can't and you know it."

His hand went to hers as he hauled her into him. "Okay, petal. You win. The dress will stay intact until we're home. Then…all bets are off."

She resisted the urge to kiss him, knowing full well that would be too much of a test to her willpower. How she got like this she still didn't know. She was pretty sure Wade had turned her into a sex-crazed beast. It was as if she couldn't get enough of him.

"Come on," she tugged at his hand, "let's go."

During the drive over to the church, her mom called again. Riley didn't answer. Her mother's calls had gone from twice a day to all day ever since she'd found out about Wade. Naively, she thought they'd eventually calm down. But two months and two weeks of having a boyfriend and her parents were still freaked out.

"You're not gonna get that?" Wade took his eyes off the road for a second to throw a concerned frown her way.

"It's my mom again." Riley sighed. "I told her I'd be busy all day with the wedding, so I don't know why she's calling."

"Maybe we should pay them another visit next week?"

Riley grimaced. Since the introduction from hell, they'd had two more painful lunches with her parents. The first to celebrate her new job, where she spent most of the time trying to convince them she was up to the task of being a chef at the Evans ranch. The second was two weeks ago. Again, it went downhill quickly when her father began inquiring about the turnover of the ranch. He then deemed it appropriate to start listing all the local ranches that had recently gone bankrupt.

"You really want to brave Silver Valley again? I think I've still got heartburn from our last visit."

Wade's dimples were paired with a short, sharp laugh. "Trust me, I'm not in a hurry to go over my latest bank statements…but they're your parents. They're important to you, which makes them important to me."

Riley didn't reply. She simply stared. He was perfect. Sweet. Kind. Funny. Not to mention the most beautiful man she'd ever seen. But beyond all that, he made her comfortable enough to just be. He didn't care that she had a habit of blurting out whatever came into her head. Or get annoyed when she didn't understand a joke and she asked him to explain. Which happened a lot.

"Why are you looking at me like that, petal?" He side-eyed her just as he pulled up into a parking space.

"I love you." She was unusually calm as she declared her love. Maybe because she'd waited so long to say it, she'd already come to terms with the fact it was likely too soon for Wade to feel the same. But that didn't matter. She just wanted him to know.

"What did you say?" His gaze swung to her, an unreadable expression hardening his face.

"I love you," she repeated, swallowing down the sudden lump in her throat.

His eyes lit. Blue fire hot enough to melt the snow covered parking lot. "You love me?" he asked again. Making her question if she'd even said the words out loud.

This time, she decided to nod in reply. Her heart hammering against pink silk as she tried her best to search him for clues.

In true Wade fashion, his reply came in the form of his mouth slamming down onto hers. He treated her to one of the claiming kisses she loved so much. Pure possession sending tingles all the way down to the tips of her toes.

The intensity didn't subside as he released her, he stayed close enough for his stubble to graze against her jaw.

"I love you too, Riley."

All the air in her lungs whooshed right on out of her.

He loves me?

She was in an alternate universe. No. She was dreaming. That was it. Any minute now, her high school math teacher was going to turn up with a surprise pop quiz she'd not studied for.

"Riley?" Wade brushed his lips against hers. "Did you hear me, baby?"

Don't worry, Mr Thomson's on his way and he's going to want you to factor quadratic equations.

"I love you," he murmured. "Being with you feels like home."

Mr Thompson wasn't coming. There was no pop quiz. The sexy cowboy making her lips wet was in love with her. And there was a strong possibility she was having a heart attack.

One problem at a time, Riley.

***

Hunter and Rachel's church ceremony was traditional, elegant, and understated. The reception, however, was the complete opposite. An explosion of pink covered the insides of the town hall. With neon signs fighting for space along the walls and fuchsia tulips decorating pink linen tablecloths.

"Jesus Christ," Matt said as he took in the cotton candy dreamscape. "You think they got a bulk discount if they ordered everything in the shop that's pink?"

"It's like someone tipped over a truckload of Pepto-Bismol." Benny was next to take in the room.

"I think it's amazing," Riley announced. "It's like Barbie's dream house."

"Yeah, on steroids." Benny's eyes were still wide as they swept around the room.

Riley smiled at Hunter and Rachel. They hadn't made an entrance to some cheesy song, instead, they'd arrived with their friends and were already on the dance floor swaying.

"It's romantic," she uttered. "Hunter would paint the whole of Woodvalley pink if it made his wife happy."

"You're right about that, petal." Wade's arms circled her waist. "What color shall I paint it for you?" A lingering kiss was planted in her hair.

"Excuse me while I throw up." Matt groaned. "I need a drink." He was halfway to the bar seconds later. Benny hot on his heels.

She twisted in his hold, her arms going around his neck

as she looked into bright blue. "Hmmm, maybe a deep purple?"

Wade's head dipped until his nose lightly nudged hers. "Done, baby."

They stayed like that for a while, breathing each other in until his woodsy scent surrounded her, every inhale more intoxicating than the last.

It was only when her hip began vibrating that the spell was broken. She didn't need to even check her phone to know it was her mother again.

"You should take it," Wade muttered.

Urgh.

Pulling the phone out of her purse, she pouted as she answered. "Hi, Mom."

"I've been trying to call you." Her mother huffed.

"I'm at the wedding I told you about, remember? I'm a bridesmaid."

The line went quiet. Riley tapped her foot impatiently while waiting, avoiding Wade's gaze that she already knew was on her.

"Right. Well, your father and I need to speak with you, are you able to drive down tomorrow?"

She could. She didn't want to. But she could. They'd taken the weekend off for the wedding which meant she wasn't working.

"Let me just ask Wade—" she was about to turn and do just that until her mother's voice stopped her in her tracks.

"No. Just you, Riley. Your father and I would like to talk to you privately."

What the hell?

"Okay," she easily agreed. If she didn't, who knew how long she'd be on the phone for. "I've got to go Mom; I'll see you tomorrow."

She wasted no time telling Wade about her parent's request as she slipped the phone back into her bag.

"Is that okay?" she cautiously asked.

"Darlin', you don't need my permission." That was true.

But she'd been looking forward to spending the whole weekend with him without work interrupting their quality time. "*Are you okay* with going up there?"

No. "It's not my first choice on how I'd like to spend my Sunday." She shrugged. "But maybe they'll ease off with the phone calls if I spend some time with them."

She very much doubted that would be the case, but a girl can dream.

***

Riley couldn't believe what she was hearing. When she'd arrived at her parent's house thirty minutes ago, she was expecting maybe a lecture on their favorite topic; personal safety. Or perhaps she'd be quizzed on her car maintenance. There was even a chance that they'd give her a belated birds and the bees talk now that she was in a relationship. But this. She wasn't prepared for this.

"Did you hear me?" Her mother's voice echoed in her ears.

How could she be sick? Her mom was the healthiest person she knew. She ate well, walked ten thousand steps a day, rarely even got a cold.

"What do they think it is?" Riley asked, hugging her glass of juice tight.

"They're still doing tests."

"So, it could be nothing?" Her voice caught.

Her mother's eyes went to her father's and then back to Riley. A silent exchange. Of what, she had no idea.

"Let's wait and see." Was all she said.

Her mother was unusually calm. So was her dad. The only one freaking out was her.

"When's your next appointment, I'll come with you?"

"Well, that's actually what we wanted to talk to you about." Riley's stomach flipped. "While I'm going back and forth to the hospital, we could use some help around the house. I won't be able to do all the things I normally do. So, we were wondering if you could take some time off, maybe come back home for a bit until we know more about what's happening?"

Take time off? Move back home? Just the idea made her want to run out of the room screaming. She finally had a life. Friends. A dream job. And a man she loved. The last thing she wanted to do was leave that all behind. She wasn't ready to give it all up.

When she didn't reply, her mother continued. "Maybe you can talk to that boyfriend of yours, work something out. It'll just be for a few months. And we wouldn't ask unless we had no other choice, you know that don't you, Riley?"

No other choice.

Guilt made her stomach churn. Other than her dad's brother, there was no other family nearby. She was all they had.

"I'll speak to Wade," she reiterated what her mother said. "The restaurant is meant to be opening in the new year, after Christmas, this month I'm supposed to be training the staff."

It was already December. A month away from opening. She didn't think her parents realized what a big deal this job was and how much responsibility she'd been entrusted with. She couldn't just pick up and leave. People were counting on her.

"Like I said, dear, we wouldn't ask unless we had to." Her mom rubbed at her eyes, there was also a loud sniff and a stern head shake. Riley watched on not knowing what to make of it. She wouldn't necessarily say the woman was cold, but she definitely wasn't into showing much emotion. Stoic. That was a good word. She was stoic. "This is hard for me and your father, Riley. We've never once asked you for anything. We've never asked you to contribute to the household financially or otherwise. But now we need you. And selfishly, I want to spend as much time as I can with you…in case…in case the worst happens."

Suddenly, she couldn't breathe. *In case the worst happens.* It felt like her mother had just plunged a knife into her heart. And then twisted it for good measure.

I need to talk to Wade.

CHAPTER EIGHTEEN

This was the problem with being a good man. There were rules. Restrictions that came with it. For example, you can't call bullshit when your girl tells you her mom's sick. Even though she hadn't been diagnosed with anything yet. Because then not only would you not be a good man, you'd also be a dick.

Just once, I'd like to be a dick.

Riley was upset. Obviously. She'd rubbed her wrist so hard; she'd left a red mark.

"Petal." He went to her. Bouncing down on his couch cushions, his hand went to her knee. "It'll be okay, I promise. We'll work something out. Together."

"They want me to move home." His jaw clenched again, like it had the first time she'd told him that. Of course they wanted her home. It was hard to control someone's life when they were a two-hour drive away.

You're being a dick.

He was. But only in his head. He was giving himself that.

"I know, baby. You haven't told me what *you* want to do though."

"I don't know." She let out a heavy sigh. "I just keep thinking about something happening and me not being there."

Wade squeezed his eyes shut and concentrated on his breathing. He needed to stay in control.

"They need me." Riley went on. "My mom does everything. She cooks. She cleans. She pays the bills. If she can't do that…then I need to step in. I need to help, because they're, well, they're my parents. I have to go back, right?"

If she was asking Wade to agree, then she was shit out of luck.

"Listen to me, darlin'." He kept his voice gentle. "You don't have to move back home to help them. Yes, you'll need to go back more often, and yes, if you want to help with money or cooking or cleaning…you can do that, too. But you have to know it's possible to do all that without moving back."

"How can I do that from here?" Doe eyes met his.

"We can do it together." His hand lifted from her knee, and he laced his fingers through hers. "We will work out your hours at the restaurant, so you have more time to go back and forth. We can bulk cook meals, freeze them and take them over to your parents so they always have food. We'll get a cleaner to go over every week for them. And financially…if they need help, we can work that out too. Together."

Her eyes went so wide that she looked like she'd seen a ghost. "I can't…you can't do that. It's not your responsibility to do all that."

"Riley, I love you. With that love comes responsibility. A responsibility to be there for that person. No matter what. Life isn't all sunshine and roses…but when you love someone, you show up."

"When you love someone, you show up," she repeated to herself quietly, her gaze hitting the floor.

Hearing her say those words out loud should have been comforting. But it wasn't. The way her voice shook made dread pool in his stomach. He knew that she was applying that logic to her mother. Letting it feed into her guilt. So it wasn't a surprise when she jumped up from the emerald loveseat and announced, "I have to move back, Wade."

Fuck.

"Because you want to?" He made sure to ask carefully.

"No. Because it's the right thing to do."

He didn't agree. Maybe it was because he could never imagine his mother asking him to make such a sacrifice. Or maybe it was because he'd witnessed firsthand how her parents manipulated her. Either way, he knew that if she went back now, it wouldn't just be for a few months. It would be forever.

Picking himself off the comfy cushions, he levelled her with the calmest stare he could muster.

"I don't believe for one second that giving up your life is the right thing to do."

Her hands shot to her hips and more dread swirled. "So you're telling me you wouldn't do the same thing for your parents if they needed you?"

"They wouldn't ask." He was quick to reply. The feeling of his nostrils flaring was a reminder his composure was slipping.

"So my parents are in the wrong for needing my help?" That was a fucking trap. Which meant he didn't reply. Which also meant, Riley went on. "Not everyone has three other siblings to share the load. I'm all my parents have."

Her voice was getting louder, while Wade's muscles were getting tighter.

"Your uncle is there," he pointed out. Regretting it the moment he witnessed steam radiate off his woman.

"Say what you need to say, Wade," she goaded. Another trap. "You obviously have an opinion on this that you're holding back."

He wasn't going to fall for that, either. "You don't need to move back home to help them, Riley. That's all I'm saying. Don't let guilt make this decision."

"Guilt? You think I feel guilty? You think that's what this is about. I'm going to help them out of guilt? Well sorry to break it to you, but you're wrong. I'm going to do it because this is what you do for family. What you do for love."

That was a lie. Not that he didn't believe a person would do what she was doing out of love. Plenty would. And did. She, however, was doing it out of guilt.

"Fine," he snapped. "Let's talk about love, darlin'. Let's talk about what happens when you love someone."

His voice rising only made the wall Riley had already put between them stronger as her facial expression hardened. It didn't deter him though. If she wanted his opinion, then she was going to get it.

"When you love someone, all you want is for them to be happy. Even if that means being without them." She wasn't getting it, so he continued. "You told me that for the first time in your life, you're happy, Riley. Here, in Woodvalley. Your parents know that too. Now think about it. Really think." He paused, giving her time to try and absorb what he was saying. "When or if you have kids—is that what you'd want for them? Knowing they were finally happy after however many years and asking them to give that up, to look after you?"

Moisture pooled in her big brown eyes. He wanted to go to her. Pull her into his arms and tell her everything was going to be okay. But the second he saw her denial blaze; he knew he'd lost her.

A moment later, she was gone.

***

"She's gone?" His mother was frowning almost as much as he was.

"She's gone," he confirmed. But the nausea hadn't.

After their discussion, he'd given her some time to cool off before heading down to her trailer. When he got there, she was gone, and so were her things.

Not knowing what to do or where to turn, he'd gone running to his mom. Over coffee and cake on her white wood deck, he'd told her everything.

He'd never been much of a sharer. He was questioning

that now. It felt good to get everything off his chest. How he felt about the woman he'd only been seeing two and a half months. His concern about Riley's parents. And everything in between.

His ma just listened. She didn't judge. She didn't interrupt. She simply nodded. But now he'd got to the end of the story, he needed more. He needed her to tell him what to do.

"So?" he asked.

"So…what?" His mother cut off another slice of orange sponge cake and pushed it onto her plate.

"What do I do?"

"You know what to do, son," she declared before taking a big bite of cake.

She was wrong. He hadn't a damn clue what to do. Which was exactly why he was there. Begging his mom for help.

When he didn't reply and likely pulled some sort of hopeless expression, her eyes flicked up in disbelief mid-chew. He waited out her eating, only to hear his mother sigh.

"Wade Evans," she hissed as a pointed finger waved in his direction. "Don't you dare sit there and pretend you don't know what to do."

What is she talking about?

"I raised you right, didn't I?" *Huh?* Another heavy exhale escaped her lips. "Okay, son. Let's try this another way. Let's pretend one of your brothers was in a similar situation and they came to you for advice…what would you suggest they do?"

"It's not the same," Wade immediately denied, knowing full well what his advice would be. His mother stayed quiet, pinning him with a no-nonsense stare as she plopped another chunk of sponge cake in her mouth and chewed. "Ma, it's not the same."

It was the same though, and he knew it. And that pissed him off again. If he'd had gone to Matt, Jonah or Zach for advice, they all would have told him the same thing, so he didn't know why he expected a different answer from his mother. She had raised them all the same. To know what love is. And what to do with it when it comes along.

"You want me to say it?" she caved. "Fine."

I should have called Matt.

At least then Wade could call him an asshole while his brother laid it all out for him. There was no way he'd call his mom an asshole unless he had a death wish.

"You fight. You claw. You don't give up," his mother continued. "You love her harder until she gets it."

Love her harder.

How the hell was he supposed to do that? Especially when she was all the way over in Silver Valley.

"You need to get creative," his mother said, already one step ahead. "You don't have to agree with her choice to do what she's doing, you just have to support her. That's what love is."

He hated the situation her parents had put her in, but his mom was right, he loved her more.

CHAPTER NINETEEN

"Riley! Can you put your phone away for one second please? This is important."

Riley's trance broke as she shook her head and slipped the phone back into her jean pocket. Her mother was wrong. This wasn't important. They were choosing a Christmas tree.

"It's hardly a matter of life or death," she sulkily muttered under her breath as she followed her parents through a tree-lined path.

A thick blanket of snow crunched under her boots. Any other year and she would have been looking forward to her trip to the Christmas tree farm. She'd be revelling in the crisp air and the waft of fresh pine and wood smoke as she wandered the maze of deep green branches dusted with snowdrops.

Instead, all she wanted to do was pull out her phone again and reread Wade's messages. It had been one week since she'd run from him. From their argument, from her job, from their relationship. He should be pissed. Livid. Cursing her name to anyone who'd listen. But he wasn't.

It didn't make sense. None of it did. Granted, she was in no way a relationship expert, but she had been pretty damn sure the argument they had resulted in them breaking up. And if that hadn't been the final nail in the coffin, her leaving without so much as a goodbye surely would have done it.

So why is he still calling me?

Despite his messages that she'd already memorised, she still didn't understand. The day after she'd returned home, she'd ignored his call. The next day, she ignored two calls. The day after that, she hit decline three times. Then the messages started. Not in an obsessive stalkerish way or anything. He'd only send her one a day and he was giving off a 'I'm here for you' vibe not a 'I know where you live', call the police kind of vibe.

On the first day his message was: *When you're ready, we need to talk, petal.*

The second day, he said: *I hope you're okay. And your mom is okay. I'm here if you need anything, baby.*

And on the third day, it was: *Thinking about you, Riley. Please call if you need me.*

Then today's message had thrown her through a loop. Unlike the others, it had arrived first thing in the morning. Also, unlike the others, it got straight to the point. And she had no idea what to do or how to feel.

Wade: I love you, Riley. I told you I'd fight to keep you. So you need to know that I'm not giving up on you or on us.

She didn't get it. He wanted to keep her so what did that mean—they'd do long distance? How long would that last? With the ranch, it's not like he could just up and move to Silver Valley. So everything hung on her shoulders; when she'd be able to move back, when her mom no longer needed her. That could be months. Or years. And that wasn't fair on either of them.

While she was struggling with that, he'd decided to confuse her even more by sending a second message.

Wade: I've sent you something, it should arrive today.

What had he sent her? And why was she itching to run home to see if it'd arrived?

"Riley!" Her mother scowled. "Are you listening to me?"

Obviously not.

When she remained quiet, her mom went on. "I

said…what do you think of this one?"

Her mother waved her hand down the length of the tall spruce she stood next to. It looked like all the others. Which is why Riley simply shrugged.

Her mother tutted and stormed off. Apparently, she wasn't a fan of her non-committal shrug. *Oh well.* With her mom out of sight, Riley pulled out her phone again to read Wade's messages.

Just one more time.

***

Riley's heart was pounding so hard she could've sworn she could hear it. Her hands were shaking, so was the piece of paper she'd been staring at for at least ten minutes.

They'd returned home with the underwhelming Christmas tree an hour ago, to the sight of Wade's package on her parent's porch. She'd wanted to tear into it straight away, but as usual her parents had other ideas and made sure to keep her busy. Once they were distracted, she'd snuck off.

Looking down at the touch bracelet on her lap, she gulped. She'd heard of them before but never seen one. They were big with long distance couples. If you pressed a button on yours, then your partner's bracelet would vibrate and vice versa. It was to let each other know you were thinking about them. Wade being Wade, she knew it wasn't just for that though. It was for her anxiety too. Every time Riley got anxious her thumb went to her wrist, and she rubbed. A coping technique she'd learned long ago. But when she was with Wade, she didn't need to do it as often, because he made her feel safe. A fact she'd shared with him one night as she lay in his arms.

Her eyes quickly darted back to the note it had arrived with and her chest tightened.

I'm only a touch away, petal. Always.

He was killing her.

ISOBEL REED

CHAPTER TWENTY

"For the millionth fucking time, we're not hiring another goddamn chef. Do you want me to say it slower? Or perhaps you assholes want me to draw you a picture?" Wade seethed.

The time had come, he was officially done. He had no patience left, especially not enough to deal with his brothers.

He didn't miss Zach, Matt and Jonah exchange a look. Or the surreptitious slide of their father's letter opener across the desk. Out of Wade's reach. His brothers were *hilarious*.

They'd been gathered in their dad's office for ten minutes now, conducting their monthly meeting. But instead of going over expenditures, all anyone wanted to talk about was Riley.

"Take a breath, man," Jonah piped in. "Unless you want Zach here to give you mouth to mouth?"

"I'm not giving him mouth to mouth." Zach chuckled.

"I thought you took an oath?" Matt's head tipped toward their eldest brother.

Jonah was the one who answered as he playfully backhanded Matt's chest. "He's off the clock. You gonna step up and take one for the team?"

"You're a fucktard." Matt's grunt was met with louder laughs from Jonah and Zach.

Fuck my fucking life.

Wade buried his face in the mahogany desk he sat in front of while his brothers continued to mock him.

Just as he was ready to reconsider stabbing his brothers with the letter opener, his wrist vibrated. Suddenly, his head shot up, his spine straightened, and his gaze went to his bracelet. Riley. She was thinking about him. Needed him.

Finally.

He'd sent her the touch bracelet over a week ago and this was the first time she'd used it. The first time he'd felt her.

His wrist vibrated again, then again. When it vibrated a fourth time, his heart skipped a beat. Hope beginning to bloom. This is what he'd been waiting for.

Quickly, he pressed down on the side button. He didn't want to keep her waiting. She had to know that he was there.

"What the hell is that abomination on your wrist?" Matt called out.

Wade didn't look up. He was too busy staring at the brushed metal band. Willing it to vibrate again. And when it did, he cracked his first smile of the day. Possibly of the week.

"Jesus Christ, it lights up too!" Jonah guffawed.

"You gonna beam us up, Scotty?" Zach sniggered.

His brothers could give him shit all night. He no longer cared. Riley was out there thinking of him. Which meant only one thing. He had to go. He had somewhere to be.

Pushing up from the desk, he didn't feel much like saying goodbye. Especially after Matt asked him if he'd got his bracelet out of a happy meal.

Bastard.

CHAPTER TWENTY-ONE

Riley could not fucking believe it. She was beyond angry. She was livid. No. Scrap that, she was enraged.

Rabid is a good one too. And wrath. I'm full of wrath.

As she unlocked the front door and pushed, she swung it so hard, it banged against the hallway wall.

Good. I hope it leaves a mark!

Hoping to scrape the paint on one of her mother's white walls may not sound very wrathful but scraping every wall in the house sounded better and better by the second.

"Riley, is that you?" her mother called from the living room. Which was her next stop.

You can do this.

Anger was all the courage she needed today. Her parents had crossed a line. And not just stepped over it slightly, no, they'd ignored the no entry sign and sped through at least three red lights.

"Why do you look like that?" her mom asked as Riley came to a standstill in front of her armchair.

Riley had no idea what she looked like, but she assumed it was a cross between pissed as hell and menacing rage.

"Remember when you told me that Dr Brown was the person who referred you to St Michael's Hospital?" Riley didn't wait for her to answer before more clipped words left her mouth. "The same Dr Brown who has been my doctor since, like, birth?"

All the color from her mother's face drained. Her lips pinched. And her eyes dropped to her lap.

"Imagine my surprise when I ran into Dr Brown today, at the Juice Hut, and asked him about all the tests you're undergoing. What do you think he said, Mom? Want to take a wild guess?"

As her voice rose, she was well aware that of her thirty years on this planet, she'd never spoken to her mother like this before. But she didn't have it in her to care. Not anymore.

The room was silent. Uncomfortably so as she watched the woman in front of her shift in the cushions.

"Why?" Was all Riley asked despite knowing the answer. She wanted to hear her say it.

It remained quiet for so long; she wasn't sure she was going to get a reply. So when her mother began to speak, her voice rang in Riley's ears.

"This is where you belong, Riley. This is your home. Your father and I—"

More ringing ensued. Enough to cause Riley's eyes to flutter closed. *This is where you belong.*

"You need to be with your family." Her mother continued. "Running around with that man, pretending to be a chef—"

"Stop!" Riley interrupted. "Just stop!"

She took it back. She didn't want to hear *the why* anymore. She felt dumb enough as it was. So much so, she wasn't even sure what upset her more. The fact that her mother had lied to get her back to Silver Valley. Or the sheer laziness of the lie. Making it pretty damn clear that she thought Riley was too stupid to work it out.

So what now?

That was the big question. Enough to cause her eyes to swell and her lips to tremble as she stood still. She'd given up everything for her mom. And as much as she wanted to, she couldn't just run back to Woodvalley and beg Wade to take her back. It wasn't right. Not after how badly she'd treated him. How could he ever forgive her? Or trust her again?

"Riley…" her mother tried but was swiftly cut off by a loud bang on the front door.

Both of their attention went to the hallway as another bang rang out. Then another. Riley was stomping out of the living room moments later, still very much in wrath mode and full of fury as she flung open the door.

What on earth?

At Wade's smile, her body immediately softened. Her wrath quickly replaced with something warmer. Calmer. The tension holding her muscles hostage only seconds ago was already melting away.

"What are you—" She didn't have time to finish that sentence because he'd already taken a step over the threshold. One hand going to her hip, hauling her into him while the other cupped her face.

"I got here as soon as I could." His voice was rough, his breaths labored as his fingers threaded through her hair. "Are you good?"

Of course he'd dropped everything for her. Wade Evans was the best man she knew. Even after everything she put him through, here he was, at her door. Showing up.

When you love someone, you show up.

Those words. His words. This time they hit differently. Her heart was leaping while her mouth dried.

"I'm sorry," she started, "I shouldn't have…I should've…" she was coming up blank. Nothing she could say felt good enough. A simple sorry sounded inadequate.

Tell him you love him.

Yes. That was it. Love. People liked hearing that. *And maybe begging?*

Just as her mouth opened again, Wade's head dipped. When his lips met hers, that was it. All thoughts melting as she easily surrendered. Words no longer seemed all that important as the world began falling away and a sense of rightness settled over her.

Lacing her fingers around Wade's strong neck, she felt herself pull him closer. Every emotion she'd spent two weeks bottling up, poured out of her as he held her close.

It was only when his thumb came to her cheek and swiped away tears that she even knew she'd sprung a leak. But he didn't break the kiss. Instead, his hand on her hip went to her back, where with one gentle press, their bodies moulded together.

She wanted to stay like this forever. Wrapped safely in Wade's hold. Breathing in the heady, masculine scent of him as the air crackled with ragged, desperate breaths. More proof of how badly they needed this.

"Who is it?" Riley ignored her mother's voice that had gotten nearer and focused on the smoky musk filling her throat.

She was finally home.

Her mother's shrill voice got even closer, but this time she had no idea what was said. Wade must have heard though, which was why he was slowing the kiss. Still, that didn't stop him muddling her mind with lip tugs and teeth scrapes.

When he finally released her, she wanted to protest. She wasn't ready for reality yet. And she certainly wasn't ready to face her mom's scowl next to her.

"Oh, I see, you call him straight after speaking with Dr Brown?" Her mother was not in any position to be making snide comments. And she was damn lucky that a mind-blowing kiss had managed to calm Riley's wrath. Or there'd be a hell of a lot of wall scraping going on round about now.

Still in Wade's big, strong arms, she shifted only slightly until she was facing her mother. "I'm done, Mom. I'm moving back to Woodvalley. It's time for me to live my life. I deserve it." She felt Wade's swift inhale at her declaration and turned back to him. *Okay. Time to beg.* "I'm sorry, Wade. I should have listened to you. And I shouldn't have left you like I did. I know I don't deserve your forgiveness but—"

"Hey," calloused hands cupped her face, "don't do that.

You deserve *everything*, petal. *Everything.*"

Her heart began to swell. "You forgive me? But what about the restaurant…what about the training I was supposed to give the staff? You're opening in a couple of weeks." Her head dipped and shook. He'd given her everything she'd ever wanted, and she'd let him down.

Wade wasn't a fan of the head dip and used his forefinger under her chin to nudge her face back up. "I couldn't give a flying fuck about the restaurant, darlin'. You. That's what I care about. *You* coming home. *You* letting me love you. You gonna let me do that?"

Home. He was it. And if he'd still have her—and it sounded a lot like he would, that's where she wanted to be.

"Yes," she breathed. "Take me home, Wade."

Those dimples engaged and bright blue eyes twinkled.

"Um, excuse me?" Her mom tapped her shoulder.

Can't she see I'm trying to have a romantic moment here?

With no chance of her reading the room anytime soon, Riley decided to give her one more thing before she packed. Just so she was clear on how things were going to go from now on.

"The daily phone calls are going to stop." Riley untangled herself from Wade, but didn't get too far as his hand shot out and curled around hers. "I'll come visit when I can. And you and dad can come to Woodvalley. Now, I'm going to go pack, and Wade is going to come help me."

She had already started dragging Wade down the hall when her mother replied, "What about Christmas?"

"I'll have to let you know what our plans are nearer the time." Riley didn't stop walking, nor did she refrain from climbing the stairs.

"But it's next week!" her mother hollered after her.

It was next week. But right now, it felt like Christmas had come early.

Wade was in her face as soon as her bedroom door slammed closed, backing her up, eyes flaring.

"Fuck, Riley," he breathed. "I missed you."

"I missed you, too."

So much it hurt. Her mother was right. As soon as she'd finished speaking with Dr Brown she'd used her bracelet.

"I don't want you moving back into the trailer."

"But…" she trailed off, her stomach twisting. She thought they were on the same page. Maybe he hadn't forgiven her after all.

This is where you beg again. And you forgot to use the L word! Get your shit together, Riley.

"Whatever you're thinking, petal, you're wrong." He smiled as fingertips skimmed her cheek. "I want you to move your stuff into the house."

"You want me to move in with you?" The question came out in a much higher pitch than she intended.

"Riley, baby, I've waited a lifetime for you. I don't want to waste any more time. I want to wake up with you every morning and go to bed with you every night." Dropping his forehead, he let his nose slowly trace hers. "Say you'll do it. Say you'll move in with me."

"But—" this was insane. It had only been three months. Yet it felt so right.

Her chest pounded as his hot breath moistened her lips. Was she really going to do this?

This time, it was her mouth that pressed against his. Teasing the seam of his lips as she coaxed him open. Giving him her answer as she took the kiss deeper, every swipe of her tongue a promise. A promise that she was his and he was hers. Always.

Yes. Christmas had definitely come early.

EPILOGUE

One week later

Riley squirmed. It was official, blindfolds were no fun outside the bedroom.

"Can I take it off now?" she asked again, her fingers already fiddling with the black cloth.

"Hold on," Wade replied. "Okay. Now. Now you can take it off."

She wasted no time ripping the material from her eyes. And when she did, she felt her smile stretch all the way to her ears as she took in the huge space.

Wow.

"It's amazing," she gushed. "You guys did so much while I was away."

The shabby chic barn had finally completed its transformation. There were no old stalls in sight, it was now a fully-fledged rustic restaurant with a sprinkling of subtle modern touches. The exposed brick and the wooden beams meant it kept its character and fitted perfectly with the reclaimed wood tables and minimalist chairs. But her favorite part was the floor to ceiling windows they'd put in by the entrance. She'd seen them being fitted but this was the first time she'd seen how well they went with the rest of the décor. And that view. Miles and miles of fields. It was magical.

"You like it?" Was he kidding? "Come, I want to show you your kitchen."

Your kitchen.

She may have swooned as he took her hand and led them through into the newly created back room. While she'd helped pick the appliances, seeing everything set up, ready and waiting for her was enough to take her breath away.

She still couldn't believe this was her real life. Her real job. Her real man. How did she get this lucky?

Twisting to face Wade, she stared up into bright blue. "Do you think your parents will mind if I spend the next twenty-four hours in here, getting to know my new oven?" she teased.

Wade flashed her those sexy dimples before pulling her into him. "It's Christmas day, darlin'. As much as I want you to bond with the kitchen appliances, I'd much rather spend our first Christmas *actually* together."

Our first Christmas.

She liked that. She liked everything about today and her new life. And even though it was still hard to grasp just how much had changed in such a short space of time, she understood why and how. Because that was what love was all about. It changed you. Forever.

***

One month later

Wade had never exactly been a social butterfly, so, him being out at a party was unusual. Well, it was until recently. Riley had become very close with Rachel, Bella, Cat and Libby, which meant he was being dragged along to many more gatherings than he was used to.

Like you don't love it.

Okay. So, love might be going a bit far. But he did like it. Mostly because seeing Riley shine was his favorite thing in the world. And shine she did. She was completely at ease in the large group of friends which included his brother Zach, and her friends' men, Hunter, Cody and Luke. Let's not forget Benny too.

That's not to say she still didn't get anxious. She did. Usually when she was around people she didn't know. Which if you asked him, was completely normal. Not that she agreed.

Today wasn't one of those days though. They were all gathered at Zach and Libby's for game night. Although they had yet to get to any games and Wade hadn't spotted any in the cosy living room where he currently stood with his beer.

"Look at you, all smiling and shit." Benny slapped him on the back. That was him. He'd turned into a smiler. Life was good. "Riley got any single friends who want a tour of Woodvalley?"

That would be a hell no.

"You run out of women in town already?" Wade teased.

He was treated to a wink. "It's a small town, man."

Wade could only shake his head. It *was* a small town so he and everyone else were well aware of Benny's inability to commit to any one woman.

"Hey, Benny." Riley smiled as she tucked herself under Wade's arm. "How did the move go?"

Benny had just bought a house. A fact he was only aware of because he'd been staying at Luke's while he waited for completion, and Luke had a big mouth. And spent the majority of Benny's time there bitching about how his friend was a cockblock.

"Good, thanks, sweetheart," Benny replied. "But could do with a woman's touch—you ever get sick of this one, you come find me." Another freaking wink.

"Seriously?" Wade's sneer was met with a full belly laugh.

Unbelievable.

Bella and Luke were the next to arrive, greeting Libby at the door with a bottle of wine. After a quick glance around, they made a beeline for Wade, Riley, and Benny, where the group had started to gather. Luke waved a stack of envelopes like a man on a mission as he strode toward them.

"Hey, douchecanoe, how many times do I need to tell you to change your address? I'm still getting all your mail, and trust me, I have no interest in hearing about your penis enlargement plans!"

The group burst out laughing as the letters were shoved into Benny's hands.

"Sorry." Bella giggled as her hand went to Luke's arm. "I'm getting him tested."

"Tested for what?" Riley asked. Not getting the joke. God, she was cute.

He couldn't help himself. He dipped down to lay a sloppy kiss in her hair and was rewarded with her bright smile.

"Save your money, sweetheart. He already tested positive to being a dick." Benny quipped.

After a while, conversation between the group faded into the background as he held Riley close.

How did I get so lucky?

He finally had it all. His dream woman. A job he loved. Actual people he considered friends. And it was only just the start. He had big plans. One of which was already burning a hole in his pocket.

"What the fuck!" Benny's usual jovial demeanour switched in an instant, bringing Wade out of his head and turning to look at the man in question.

He'd been opening his mail, and one particular letter had caught his attention. In a bad way. But Wade suspected it wasn't just an unwelcome bill. There was too much tension thickening the air.

Bella, Luke and Riley all asked, "What?" But their question went unanswered as Benny continued to stare at the small card in his hand. Then he was gone. Storming through the arch leading to the kitchen and then slamming the back door. Not before chucking the mail onto the countertop.

Riley was off. Following his footsteps and retrieving whatever he'd been holding before coming to a stop.

My little detective.

She bit down on her lip as she passed the card to him.

Wade looked down at the wedding invite, Benny's anger no longer a mystery.

So the rumors he'd heard were true. Not only was Benny's old high school sweetheart back in Woodvalley. She was getting married. And apparently, Benny had been invited.

God help Woodvalley Pines. The past was back...and she was wearing a white wedding dress.

SNEAK PEEK AT BOOK SIX IN THE LOVE BURNS SERIES

Hitched

You're going to hell Bethany. Straight up, Lucifer shoving pokers up your ass, hell.

"You had to go for the ball gown wedding dress, didn't you?" Bethany tutted to herself.

To be fair, at the time, she had no idea she would be trying to cram four layers of tulle out the bathroom window. In hindsight, a simple A-line would have been more suitable for this kind of thing.

Are you seriously thinking about runaway bride attire right now?

She was. Anything was better than thinking about what she was actually doing.

Finally free of the much smaller than she thought, bathroom window, she felt her heels sink into the freshly cut grass.

"Okay. Now what? Call an Uber?" She muttered to herself as her eyes darted around the church yard. Thank God everyone was inside. Well. Almost everyone.

Shit!

Before she'd even had a chance to gather her dress and realize that her heart was in her throat, the man in the black fitted suit was walking toward her. Their gazes locked.

Shit. Shit. Shit.

"What the hell are you doing?" The man hollered as he continued in her direction.

The nerve. He had no right to be angry.

"You're still smoking?" Was her haughtily reply.

"What?"

"You're still smoking?" She repeated. "Don't you know those things will kill you?"

Way to pull off self-righteous mid-way through ditching your wedding, Bethany.

"That's what you wanna to talk about right now?" He scoffed, coming to a halt just close enough to remind her of his familiar forest scent. "Not the fact that you just climbed out of that window behind you?" Benny pointed to the cloudy, rippled glass over her shoulder.

"Did you bring your truck?" she asked with a tilt of her head.

"What?"

"Your truck, Benny, did you bring it?" She let out an exasperated sigh.

His look was beyond suspicious, "of course I brought my truck, Beth, I didn't fucking fly here."

Fucking smartass. Some things never change.

Beggars can't be choosers.

"Well, what are we waiting for? Let's go!" Her hand was in his seconds later as she hurriedly dragged him across the abandoned courtyard.

Just when she didn't think this day could get more fucked up, she was gathering four layers of tulle again and cramming it into her ex-boyfriend's old pickup truck.

Fuck you too universe.

Benny climbed in next to her, not hiding the dirty looks he was casting as he started the old banger. And it was an old banger. He'd been driving the faded red beast at least a decade. She remembered when he'd first got it, the paint was still shiny then, and you could make out the two-tone design on the bench seat fabric, now, not so much.

Her eyes darted to the threadbare cloth, then to the cracked dashboard as the truck rumbled to life. "Nice to know your fear of commitment doesn't extend to everything in your life." She muttered under her breath.

Benny's head snapped her way. Dark green eyes narrowing on her. "You got something you wanna say, B?"

"Oh I don't know, maybe, hurry the hell up!" She impatiently huffed, her arms crossing over her chest. "If you haven't noticed, I'm kind of in a rush?"

She didn't know why she was so mad at him. Actually, scrap that. She knew. She was annoyed he was there to witness the shitshow that is her life. Pissed he'd had the audacity to show up to her wedding. And to top it all off, she was angry as hell that he still looked so damn fine.

Nine years had been kind to Benny. His boyish features had matured. His toned body had turned muscular. His wild chestnut hair, tamed. Even the bump in his nose he'd got when someone slammed open the locker door next to him, looked rugged paired with day old stubble.

Men suck.

"I'm sorry I'm not living up to your getaway driver standards, B!" He snorted. "Maybe you want to explain to me what the fuck is going on?"

That's definitely not something she wanted to do. At least they were moving.

"Or whereabouts I'm taking you?" He pressed when she remained quiet.

She didn't have an answer for that either. Running out on her wedding wasn't on her list of things to do today. Right now, she was supposed to be Mrs Douglas Wright. But she couldn't. Staring at her reflection in that bathroom mirror, it had hit her like a ton of bricks. Her nausea wasn't nerves. The tightness in her chest on the drive over wasn't anticipation. And the churn in her stomach certainly wasn't butterflies.

The adrenaline was waning though, which meant she had to start feeling. It's why her eyes fluttered shut at the first sign of stinging.

"B?" Benny called out.

Hello? I'm trying not to cry here!

Hearing her first love's voice really wasn't helping. It was no wonder the tears won.

"Hey?" Benny's voice gentled. "NeNe, baby, you okay?"

The use of his nickname for her was enough to jolt her and possibly push her over the edge.

"No, I'm not okay. I just ran out on my wedding. My

FREAKING wedding!" Her voice might have risen. "I have nowhere to go 'cause my parents will be pissed as hell I've ran out on a wedding they paid for. I can't go back to my apartment 'cause the man I just left standing at the alter lives there. And if that's not enough of a shit sandwich, I'm currently sitting in a big-ass white wedding dress in a truck I not only lost my virginity in, but with the man who fucking took it – with no money, no clothes and no idea what the hell I'm going to do. So no. I'm not o-fucking-kay."

She threw her head back, loudly sighing as it met metal. She forgot there was no headrest. *You don't deserve a headrest.* No. She didn't. She needed to prepare for discomfort before her trip to hell.

You might have already arrived.

Unsurprisingly, her rant was met with silence, which she was taking as a good thing. It's not like there was much to say. And she could use this time to figure out some sort of plan.

DON'T MISS THE REST OF THE BOOKS IN THE LOVE BURNS SERIES

Toasted

Welcome to Woodvalley Pines...where hunky firefighters save the day! It's time to turn up the heat and hope this smokin' hot fireman can control the blaze.

Libby hadn't even been in Woodvalley Pines a day and she was already freaking out. Her kitchen had just set on fire. From toast of all things! That's right, she was the victim of the elusive toaster fire. Yes, a toaster. Who knew they could just spontaneously burst into flames? She certainly didn't. If that wasn't enough to ruin her day, a swarm of hot firefighters seeing her in her pink pajamas would do it.

Zach tried his hardest not to laugh as the woman in the Disney pajamas accused him of keeping toaster fire safety a secret. He didn't know where in the world this angry green-eyed princess had come from, but he had to admit that he was intrigued. After all, if she had this much passion when it came to talking toasters, what other kind of flames could he stoke in her?

Libby and Zach's spark was instant, but will the fire burn out or can they keep the flames blazing?

Isobel Reed's snarky humorous romances have fans fanning themselves as they devour the stories. Her books are one-clicks for readers who love Lori Wilde's - The First Love Cookie Club and Jennifer Ryan's - At Wolf Ranch books. Readers will struggle not to fall for the sexy small town heroes and the sassy women who claim them!

EXCERPT:

"You okay, ma'am? Neighbor reported he heard screaming."

Oh shit.

"Oh, yeah. There was screaming. I mean, yes, I did scream. But it was more like a release, y'know? Like, when you're having a really shitty day and you scream into a pillow. It was kinda like that." *For the love of God, stop talking.* "Anyway, yeah, I'm fine. All good. Hunky-dory."

Hunky-dory? Really? And screaming into pillows? Way to embarrass yourself in front of the handsome firefighters. Are your Disney pajamas not enough humiliation for you? Do you want to detail your hair removal regime next?

Luckily, the other man decided not to comment. He simply nodded, for which Libby was grateful. Once he'd given Zach a quick update on the cause of the fire – that blasted toaster – he disappeared and left the two of them alone again.

Turns out, just the mention of the toaster was enough to bring back her rage.

"Did you know toasters just sometimes set on fire? When exactly did that become a thing? And why aren't there more people talking about it?"

Zach incorrectly thought that clearing his throat would be enough to mask his snigger. "Uh, well, any old appliances can be a potential fire hazard. With toasters, a build-up of breadcrumbs can also act as fuel to the fire."

"What the hell? I didn't know that, Zach. Why didn't I know that? Is this some big firefighter secret or something? 'Cause I'm telling you right now, people need to know this! I'm thirty-one, Zach. *Thirty-one!* And never in my life would I have thought I could be making toast one day and then ... *boom!* Fire! People need to be told. They need to know, damnit!"

Okay, it was safe to say this was not her finest moment. She was well aware ranting about toaster fires while sitting on the curb – in just her miniscule, bright pink shorts and vest top – was giving off batshit crazy vibes. But she clearly just couldn't help herself. Once she got a look at his expression, the crazy continued.

"Are you laughing at me?"

"No, ma'am."

"You are ... you're laughing at me!"

"Smiling. I'm smiling at you. There's a big difference."

Cop-Off

Return to Woodvalley Pines…where a sexy police officer comes across one troublemaker that he's determined to pin down.

Cat is looking to snag herself a cowboy. After all, what else is there to do in the small town of Woodvalley Pines. And after the year she's had, she deserves to treat herself. There's only one problem. Cody freaking McBride. The devil himself. And the bane of her existence. It's bad enough she has to look at his smug face most days, but now he's made it his mission to meddle in her love life. Which means only one thing, it's about to get ugly.

Single dad and local cop Cody thought he was done with love. He was content in his routine. Work, eat, sleep, repeat. But then Cat shows up in town. Lighting fires wherever she goes and hurling insults his way while she's doing it. He actually finds himself enjoying fighting with the little she-devil, it's the most alive he's felt in years.

Woodvalley Pines is about to witness the ultimate showdown. Where clothes aren't the only things getting torn to shreds.

Cop-Off is set in a small town filled with sassy heroines, hunky heroes, and busybodies who can't help but share their two cents. Fans of Any Man of Mine by Rachel Gibson and Worth the Risk by Jamie Beck will love Isobel Reed's steamy, snarky romance!

EXCERPT:

"You cannot write that!" Libby gasped, handing Cat back her phone.

"Why not?"

"Because you're going to attract the wrong kind of man!"

Why her friend seemed so horrified, Cat had no idea. All she'd done was show her the profile she'd set up on a local dating app. It had been Libby's idea to get back out there in the first place. That was exactly what she was doing.

"Look, Lib, I love you, but you drag me all the way out here to the middle of nowhere to, what, sit around all day? If I'm gonna be surrounded by nothing but cows, I might as well find myself a cowboy to shag."

And she *was* in the middle of nowhere. Woodvalley Pines, Wyoming was a long way from her home in Brighton, England. This hadn't exactly been what she imagined when she'd thought about moving back to America. The last time she was here, she'd been living in San Francisco, where she'd first met Libby. And she had to admit she missed the city. The hustle and bustle. Nights out. Takeout whenever you wanted it. The most exciting thing that had happened since moving to Woodvalley was the day Mrs Tucker lost her cat. For an hour.

"A dating profile full of innuendos is not gonna find you a cowboy. It's gonna find you a horny psychopath." Libby obviously wasn't done yet.

"You're being dramatic."

"Cat, at one point you wrote: *Before I take a long ride, I like to make sure my stud has had a good twenty minute warm up.*" Her best friend's eyebrow was raised, causing her to look all accusatory.

"What?" Cat not-so-innocently lifted her bare shoulder in a shrug. "That's just good horsemanship, Lib. You don't want him to be too stiff." She added a wink specifically to get a laugh out of her. And it worked.

Baked

When danger comes to the small town of Woodvalley Pines, Hunter vows to become the protector of local bakery owner, Rachel. But when things heat up, can this firefighter handle the burn?

Rachel was finally happy. She had a place to call home, amazing friends, and a successful bakery. Then her past found her. Now Hunter Campbell was in her kitchen, acting like a caveman. After months of only grunting at her, one little incident, and he has the audacity to tell her she's not allowed out without him. She couldn't decide what terrified her more about her new bodyguard – the giant hulk scaring off her customers, or the fire in her belly that made her heart race every time he was near.

Local firefighter Hunter was a man of few words. But if ever there was a time to talk, it was now. Rachel was in danger and there was no way he was going to let anything happen to his stubborn little fairy. It didn't matter that he'd spent months keeping his distance. Or that she had the power to shatter his heart and then stab him to death with the shards. This was happening. She could bang as many baking pans as she liked. He wasn't going anywhere. She was stuck with him.

Fighting fires was nothing new to Rachel or Hunter, but surrendering to the heat of the flames was a battle neither of them were prepared for.

Isobel Reed's stories delight and bring laughter to romance through sizzling dialogue and fast-paced writing. Fans of Hot Stuff by Carly Phillips or Rescue Me by Susan May Warren will love this sassy tale of a caveman fireman and the baker who wins his heart.

EXCERPT:

Striding down the terracotta cobbles like a man on a mission, Hunter knew what most people saw as they crossed the street to avoid him. But just because most people compared his physical build to the Hulk, it didn't mean he also had the whole wrath thing going on too. Although, if he was ever going to suddenly develop anger issues, this week would have done it.

He was pissed as hell. Nine months he'd stayed away. Kept his distance. Damn well tortured himself. And all for nothing. Because now? Now he didn't have a choice. There would be no staying away anymore. Not while Rachel was in danger. It changed everything.

What kind of man would he be if he let something happen to the woman he'd not been able to stop thinking about since he first laid eyes on her, just because he couldn't get over himself?

A shit one.

Exactly. He was fine being many things. A man of few words. A man most people had to stretch their necks to see fully. He was even fine being a man who tipped the loneliness scale a bit too enthusiastically. But he drew the line at being a shit one.

That being said, he knew what going to her meant. He wasn't dense. There had been a reason he'd stayed away. A good one. And now he was willingly throwing himself into the fire.

It meant he was done running. Done fighting his feelings. It was time to claim his honeybun. It was time to claim Rachel. And that's exactly what he was on his way to do.

Stopping outside the pastel pink storefront, his eyes went to the even pinker neon sign that hung above the window display. The name Fairy Baked was flashing above a line of pretty cupcakes that had been sprinkled with assorted candy.

You've got this. Just go inside and calmly explain that starting from today, she is not to go anywhere without an escort.

Easy.

Hothead

When a sexy fireman and a sassy filmmaker's worlds collide, can they stand still long enough to let love ignite, or will their instinct to run keep them from the one thing worth fighting for?

Luke Cappelli is the ultimate bachelor. He's never stuck around longer than one night, and no woman has ever tempted him to. *Until Bella.* With a face that rivaled an angel's and a mouth that could make a sinner blush, it was like she was created especially for him. Which is why committing to a few weeks of fun felt easy. But when it came time for her to leave, Luke realized letting her go wasn't just hard—it was impossible.

Bella had one job. Deliver a letter: that's it. Easy. She'd be in and out of Woodvalley Pines faster than you could say "howdy". Well, that was the plan anyway. Until she came face to face with broody firefighter, Luke Cappelli. With a sarcastic remark for every occasion and enough red flags to fill a parade, the man had heartbreaker written all over him. It didn't matter, though, because their time together had an expiry date, which was for the best. Wasn't it?

Fans of <u>Not the Marrying Kind</u> *by Kathryn Nolan or* <u>Hot in Here</u> *by Sophie Renwick will be enthralled by Isobel Reed's sassy romances with witty dialogue and swoon-worthy happily-ever-afters. Grab a tall glass of water, find a cozy spot, and dive into HOTHEAD—a romance too sizzling to put down!*

EXCERPT:

Collapsing into the bottom bunk, he let his head drop into his hands. Marco couldn't have been more than a few years older than him. Late thirties were no age to die. What the hell happened?

Maybe you should have read the letter and found out, dumbass. Or better yet, ask the fucking angel outside.

Speaking of. Just a second later, the door swung open, causing his head to shoot up.

Okay. Maybe she's not outside anymore.

"You always walk away from people mid-conversation, Luke … or am I special?" she scolded.

She was special all right. "You always walk into rooms with big ass *Do Not Enter* signs on them … or am I just lucky?"

A genuine sigh left those sweet red lips, enough to make him regret snapping back. "Look, I get this is hard for you. Believe it or not, I understand. My family are as dysfunctional as they come. Think the Lohans … on meth. So, trust me, I get it."

Seriously, who the hell is this girl?

Rising from the bed, his feet were moving toward her before his brain had a chance to catch up. Only fully registering when nerve endings began lighting up as he sucked down more berries.

Before he knew it, he'd invaded her space. Personal bubble officially popped as his head bowed and their mouths lined up. All it would take was one small dip and he'd know for sure if those lips tasted as sweet as the woman who owned them smelled.

"Why are you here, Bella?"

He noticed her breath quicken. "Marco asked me to come." She rushed out. "To give you the letter and …"

"And what?"

"And h-he wanted me to stick around for a while."

He ignored the hammering of his heart at her declaration. His body couldn't be trusted.

"And why would he want you to stick around?"

"Are you going to take the letter?"

"You always answer questions with questions?"

Luke felt her breath warm his skin and found himself wishing away his stubble. He wanted to feel her sink into every inch of him.

Yeah. That's normal.

"Is this the proximity you conduct all your conversations?" was her reply.

It looked like he'd met a fellow smartass. The first one to drag a smile out of him.

This chick is something else.

AVAILABLE IN EBOOK AND PRINT WHERE BOOKS ARE SOLD

ABOUT THE AUTHOR

Isobel was born and raised in London. While she's a city girl at heart, she loves daydreaming about running away to a charming small town—though she's not entirely sure her husband and son would share her enthusiasm for the move. When she's not writing small-town romantic comedies or growing unhealthily attached to the characters in her books, you can find her reading, chasing after her very active toddler, or attempting to channel her inner domestic goddess in the kitchen (with varying degrees of success).

Known for her witty dialogue and swoon-worthy small-town heroes, Isobel signed with Inkspell Publishing in 2021. The following year, she released Love Tools, the first book in her four-book Bluestone Series. In early 2024, she launched Toasted, the debut novel of her seven-book Love Burns Series, which will roll out over the next year.

https://www.tiktok.com/@isobelreedbooks
https://www.facebook.com/isobelreedbooks
https://www.instagram.com/isobelreedbooks/
https://www.isobelreed.net/
https://www.amazon.com/author/isobelreed
https://www.goodreads.com/Isobel_Reed
https://www.bookbub.com/authors/isobel-reed